THE FEELER

A SCIENCE FICTION COZY MYSTERY - BOOK 1

KATHERINE OKIA

AGWANG PRESS

For my darling daughter, Marta
For my supportive husband, Peter

CONTENTS

CHAPTER 1

Coraline Brimble woke from a deep sleep with a sharp headache. As the pain faded, she recognized the subtle attack. After a quick check of her mental shield, which kept her mind safe, she took a deep breath and calmed. She had an idea who'd attacked her, but she needed to be sure. She lowered her shield in tiny increments and used her Feeler ability to probe her family home. Feelers could sense other people's emotions. She reached out with her mind, searching her floor, which included seven bedrooms and the storage space above.

Nothing.

She probed the lower floor, which consisted of two sitting rooms, a sunroom, and the dining room. She gasped as she sensed his mind and hurried to shield hers again.

"They're already in the dining room—I must be late," she said with a dry mouth. Glancing at the gentle glow next to her bed, which read fifteen minutes to ten, she sat bolt upright. "I'm very late!" She sprang to her feet. "Haley, lights," Cora said, addressing her family's home artificial intelligence. The AI was the central nervous system of the house as it maintained temperature, water and food distribution, and general cleanliness.

She squinted at the bright lights as she raced through her room, which resembled a small apartment with a dining table, office table, sofa, and bathroom. She reached the sonic shower, which removed dirt by inaudible sound vibrations. This wasn't her favorite way to start the day—she preferred the warm water of a shower, but it took more time, which she didn't have. This morning, she needed to be at breakfast by ten. A moment later, she dashed out of the sonic shower, and threw on a coordinated gray-blue top and pants set, her usual attire for business meetings. She liked the way the shirt complimented her dark-brown eyes. She rapidly smeared on her makeup, which smoothed her caramel-colored skin and ran her fingers through her unruly curly dark-brown hair, just barely taming it.

Reaching for her comm bracelet, she snapped it on her wrist. This bracelet connected her to the Global High-Frequency Network known as the Net, which allowed Earth citizens to communicate with each other, receive credits or electronic money for shopping, enjoy entertainment, create businesses, and much more. The bracelet also worked with her home's internal network. She selected a few buttons that directed her bed to make itself, the small dining table to recycle plates and food, and a small robot to tidy her shoes and clothes into the closet.

At ten, Cora stepped toward the door and felt a painful prick against her shield. She gritted her teeth with his second attack and considered poking *his* mind. A second later, she dropped the idea—it wouldn't end well for either of them.

"Why is he always like that?" she said through gritted teeth.

"I don't have enough information. Please rephrase the question." Haley spoke in a level, detached voice.

"I'm not talking to you," Cora said with an edge in her voice. After a moment, she took a deep breath. "No. I won't let him get to me. I'll just have to be late." She spoke to herself in as confident a voice as she could muster.

Cora stepped out the door of her bedroom, marched down the hall, and rushed down the stairs. Leaping across the main hall, she forgot her earlier resolve to remain calm. She almost burst through the dining room doors, but at the last minute, she reminded herself to stop and gather herself. She didn't want to show weakness because her cousin was on the other side.

"So sorry I'm late," she said, gliding into the room with a serene expression on her face. A large oval table that could seat twelve people dominated the space. This morning, only three people sat at one end of the table.

Decorated by Cora's mom while she was alive, the room reflected a subdued elegance with a repeating leafy pattern painted white on the ceiling which complemented a light sage color on the walls. The dining room table supported four unobtrusive meal crafters, which rearranged food molecules from the kitchen pantry and transported entire meals to the table. These crafters lined the center of the oval table, somewhat hidden by four bouquets of fresh flowers. The room was in the center of the house and had no windows, but its walls displayed beautiful images of gardens gathered over two generations of Brimbles hosting countless dinner parties.

"Good morning, cousin. Aren't you glad I woke you?" Oliver Robertson chuckled. He was her first cousin on her mom's side. He, like her sister Sophia, had inherited the characteristic Brimble traits that included striking attractiveness, laughing emerald eyes, dark-brown curly hair that he kept short, a flawless caramel complexion, and a tall athletic frame. Somehow, Cora had missed most of these qualities with her dark-brown eyes and short, slender frame.

"No," Cora said in a crisp tone, taking a seat across from Oliver while maintaining his steady gaze. "I don't enjoy waking up like that."

"Now, now, children. Let's not fight." Aunt Ferna Robertson, sitting next to her son Oliver, spoke as if talking to preschoolers instead of almost thirty-something adults. As Cora's mom's older sister, she was around Cora's height, a little round, and had curly gray hair.

Cora grimaced with frustration—she hated the way Aunt Ferna never seemed to notice

Oliver's misbehavior. She wished for the hundredth time that she'd been born with stronger abilities like her sister, Sophia. If she'd been stronger, she would've been able to defend herself, and her parents would've never sent her away to a boarding school 'for her own protection', as her parents had often told her.

She reached for the meal crafter and selected her usual breakfast. A cup of coffee and a plate of synthetic eggs and bacon materialized on the table. Synthetics, animal products made in specialized factories, were seen as a cleaner and more humane alternative to farming animals.

Oliver smirked. "Mom, I haven't been a child for decades." He glanced at Cora. "Even old Cora's getting up there." He chortled and took a sip of tea.

"Nonsense! She hasn't had her thirtieth birthday yet." Aunt Ferna reached for the crafter and selected her usual breakfast. A moment later, toast, jam, biscuits, and a cup of tea materialized on the table in front of her. "That reminds me. Your birthday is in a few days. Have you thought of a fun restaurant to celebrate?"

Cora's irritation melted as she remembered her tenth birthday on an overcast, snowy October alone in her dorm room. She had been away at a boarding school that she liked, but it was on the other side of the world—she had missed her family. Her parents had sent a message earlier to say that they couldn't visit for her birthday, and she couldn't come home for the December holidays. This meant she wouldn't see any family until March for the Spring holidays, and large tears had rolled down her cheeks. When an unexpected but familiar voice called, "Cora dear, where're you?" she had sprung to her feet, wiped the tears from her cheeks, and bolted to the door. She spotted her Aunt Ferna balancing a load of packages as she made her way down the hall. Suddenly, everything changed as Cora raced down the hall and hug-attacked her aunt. Every year after that, Aunt Ferna had made the long trek to her school to share her special day.

"I'm interested in trying that Martian restaurant," Cora said, coming back to the here-and-now as an inquisitive look crossed her face. "I still think it must be some sort of scam or hoax, but so many people've praised it."

Aunt Ferna grinned. "I know. I'm dying to find out. But I don't think there's anything wrong. They simply grow the food in Martian soil."

"But when you think about it, plants from Earth haven't adapted to Martian soil. So, they must have to add back some of the nutrition the plants need."

"Well, possibly. It doesn't change the fact that they're grown in Martian soil."

"Mother, I think you've missed the point." Oliver rolled his eyes.

Cora set her mouth in a disapproving line, bothered by the way Oliver treated his mom. She ignored him and turned to Harold Albright, her sister's husband, before she had passed about a year ago. Even though he was Cora's brother-in-law, he behaved more like a father. He was a tall, imposing man who was muscular in his youth, but he'd since grown some extra girth and jowls. He was almost twenty years older than Cora. "How did you sleep, Harold?"

"Well..." Harold's eyebrows furrowed with worry.

"Do you still want to meet later?" Cora asked in a soft voice. Something had worried Harold these past few weeks. After Aunt Ferna, he was the only family member who treated her with kindness and without judgment. When Cora was twenty-five, her parents had passed away in an accident, and she had faced a decision about her life. She'd always wanted to launch her own game, but her parents had been against it. Harold guided her as she worked through the difference between what she wanted and what she felt her parents expected of her. His gentle words encouraged her by teaching her that she'd owed nothing to her parents who were gone, or Sophia, an uncaring sister. Later, she'd begun coding her game, experiencing genuine happiness about her career.

He lowered his voice. "Do you have time this afternoon?"

"Yes, of course." Cora glanced at his face, marred by fear and misery. "What's this about?"

"I'll tell you this afternoon," Harold said with a small smile as he patted her hand. He munched on toast with extra jam and tea. She wished she could risk lowering her shield and sense his emotions, but she didn't dare with Oliver around. Having to use her shield among her family made her feel blind.

Cora, Aunt Ferna, and Harold ate in silence for several minutes while Oliver sipped tea and surveyed a painting.

"Cousin, have you noticed how similar you are to Grandma?" Oliver asked with a smirk. "She had no abilities, right, Mom?"

Cora turned pink. Growing up, Oliver and Sophia had enjoyed reminding her about her weak abilities. Together, they found a million ways to imply she wasn't a real Brimble because of it.

It was the year twenty-three fourteen, and for the past two or three generations, some humans had begun to change. Some scientists speculated it could be rapid evolution and others thought it was a toxin in the water. About ten percent of all humans now possessed special abilities and were called Askovians. Although the same ability occurred within a family, not all family members developed Askovian powers. In addition, these powers varied in strength between Askovian family members. Cora could sense other people's emotions and shield her mind from other people. However, Sophia and Oliver could sense and manipulate others' emotions, making them feel things that weren't real.

"Now, I called this family meeting to correct a problem." Aunt Ferna started as if Oliver hadn't just tried to humiliate Cora again.

Cora ignored Oliver and focused on Aunt Ferna's words. She nibbled her bottom lip, worried about the conversation.

"Yes, Ferna. What is it?" Harold spoke in a clipped voice—as if he also knew what Aunt Ferna wanted.

"Poor Oliver is very low on funds since you halted his regular income," Aunt Ferna said. "I think Oliver should move into this house—just until he gets back on his feet." Aunt Ferna spoke in a firm voice and peered at Harold as if challenging him.

Cora held her breath. She loved her aunt, but she'd never live in the same house as Oliver.

"Absolutely not!" Harold erupted. "I know he's your son. But..." He paused, weighing his words.

"Yes? What were you going to say?" Aunt Ferna asked in a shrill voice.

"Your son is a thief! He's spent his inheritance, and now he's trying to spend your credits. After that, he'll begin selling the valuable art and furniture from this house." Harold shook his head, causing his jowls to quiver. "I have a duty to this family to keep everyone safe from threats, and that includes your son."

"You have a duty? You're not a real Brimble, you just married in," Aunt Ferna spat. "I'm the most senior Brimble and have more say over who can stay. *Oliver stays.*"

"I'm a Brimble in every sense of the word. If Sophia and I had children, would you claim they weren't real Brimbles?" Harold huffed like a bull, ready to charge.

"Hold on. Mom. Harold." Oliver spoke with a solemn tone.

Cora lowered her shield and focused on Oliver. She sensed his radiated merriment at the turmoil he'd caused. She quickly raised her shield, noticing the difference between his facial expression and his broadcast emotions.

"Actually, after Sophia passed, this home became Cora's. Mom, you get it after Cora." Oliver turned to Cora. "Are you comfortable with me living here?"

Three sets of eyes bored into her.

Cora felt a heavy weight settle on her shoulders. She loved Aunt Ferna and looked up to Harold—they both treated her like a daughter. For the first time in her life, her family felt complete, and she couldn't choose one over the other. She glanced at the door, wanting to run away. Finally, she decided to go with the truth. She shifted in her seat, trying to hide her discomfort as she faced Aunt Ferna with a gentle smile. "I'm very sorry Aunt, but I can't live here with Oliver."

Aunt Ferna set her jaw and drew her lips into a straight line. "Well... Well, if that's how you feel."

Oliver leaned toward his mom and hugged her, but Cora caught his smirk, which saved her from guilt. He enjoyed the drama he'd caused.

"It's alright, Mom. I think I have a simple solution." Oliver's face twitched as he tried to fight off a grin.

"Yes, what is it?" Aunt Ferna huffed.

"I love living in Lunar City and don't really want to move." Oliver glanced at Harold. "In a couple of days, I start my new job. I just need a few credits to tide me over until then."

Cora raised an eyebrow. She'd never known Oliver to hold a job longer than a couple of weeks.

"Are you sure, dear?" Aunt Ferna asked in a hopeful tone. "I miss you so much when you're away."

"I know, and I miss you," Oliver said with a little more sincerity. "Also, I'll need a ticket for the Lunar shuttle."

"When're you going to send Oliver his credits?" Aunt Ferna asked, but it sounded more like a command than a question.

"First, they aren't Oliver's credits," Harold furrowed his eyebrows. "They're your credits, and you need to take better care of your inheritance." Harold sighed. "Second, I've arranged a ticket ready for a Lunar shuttle this afternoon, and I've prepared a packet of credits. You'll receive the credits once your shuttle takes off."

Aunt Ferna looked so upset that Cora wished she could lower her shield and sense her emotions. She used her ability to understand the depth of other people's emotions. Unfortunately, she'd need to leave her shield lowered longer to sense her aunt's emotions in depth, and Oliver would take advantage of her vulnerable mind.

"So, what's your new job?" Cora asked, trying to lighten the mood.

"Oh, a friend helped him get a job in a casino," Aunt Ferna bragged, preventing Oliver from answering. "He'll have a steady income and be able to afford an apartment." She turned to him with a fond smile. "You know he's so resourceful."

"Mom, you're making me blush," Oliver said, and his gaze roamed to the door as if he wanted to leave.

Cora read between the lines with ease. Oliver must have started gambling, had a good winning streak, and then lost everything—the real reason he needed funds to tide him over.

"Now you promise, no gambling?" Aunt Ferna spoke in a chiding voice.

Oliver nodded with a grim face. "I give you my solemn oath."

"Well then, it's all set." Aunt Ferna grinned at her beloved.

Cora breathed a sigh of relief.

CHAPTER 2

Cora's family home was located in the middle of a swanky residential neighborhood. The mini-mansion was shaped like a three-story white block that displayed fashionable, understated elegance with decorative white trim around every window. The entrance to the home featured a simple wooden door, which created a pleasant contrast with the lighter house colors. The manor included a vast manicured garden in the back and a modest lawn in the front.

With the unpleasant breakfast meeting over, Cora stepped out the front door and headed toward the family car Haley had brought around for her. Floating over the lawn, the white oval-shaped car had a flat top and curved windows that allowed a three-hundred-and-sixty-degree view. The automated door opened as she approached. Once inside, she lowered herself onto one of the two U-shaped sofas and leaned on the semi-circle table in the center of the car while running her hands through her hair. As much as she loved her aunt, today she felt relieved to leave the house. With Oliver there for the rest of the day until he left for his shuttle, Cora wanted to be as far away as possible.

A moment later, the car lifted into the air and Cora leaned back in her seat, gazing at the Krega Mountains, a permanent and dominant feature of Tymal City. The city rested on a vast plateau halfway to the highest peak of the Krega Mountain range. Without intervention, Krega's landscape contained sparse vegetation and snowy peaks for six months of the year. However, Tymal's inhabitants used weather technology controlled by the Weather Bureau on their tableland to create a perpetual spring for farmland, large grassy meadows, parks, and several small contained wooded areas. Cora loved gazing at the color combinations in the many fields of flowers below as she floated toward the business complex that housed the computers for her game, Mystery Adventures.

Twenty minutes later, Cora's car drifted out of the sky and landed on a grassy parking space just outside of her office. Since she had borrowed the family car, it lifted back into the sky and returned home once she stepped out.

Cora took a deep breath and felt the tension trickle away. Normally, she didn't enjoy flying to the deserted building. Something about it always gave her an eerie feeling, as if being watched. Most business owners sharing the building worked elsewhere, only occasionally visiting the building to troubleshoot problems, create products in a secure space, or store equipment. Today, she needed refuge from Oliver, and Mystery Adventures provided the perfect respite.

A small smile spread across her face as she approached the entrance to the building and stepped into the security booth. The building boasted the most advanced security measures that business owners like her required. Normally, she stepped into the booth and waited one or two seconds before it opened again. Not this time.

"Alert! Nanobots detected. Potential spyware," an electronic voice rang through the booth.

"What? Do you mean medical microscopic robots?" Cora said with an exasperated sigh. She assumed some could've dropped from the last person to enter the booth—it was unlikely, though.

"Negative. Detected nanobots not in database."

"You've malfunctioned. Run a self-diagnostic."

"Self-diagnostic complete. All systems functional. Rescanning." The electronic voice spoke in a cool, detached voice. "Clear. No spyware detected."

The booth opened, and she entered the building. Turning back to survey the booth, her eyebrows knit together as she wondered what had happened—the booth rarely malfunctioned.

She turned and paced down a long plain hallway with white walls and endless gray doors. Each door opened to a business that, for various reasons, needed space for role-playing, extra computing, testing, material storage, and more.

In a few minutes, she reached her door, which slid open, and a rush of air caressed her face. After a moment, her nose got used to the faint metallic smell as she stepped into her computer lab. It contained a wall of small windows to her left and a set of six large desks corralled in

the center of the room, each with a comfortable chair. She turned to her right, heading for
the meal crafter. A few minutes later, she sank
into a chair at the desk closest to the windows,
cradling a steaming cup of coffee, and sighed
contentedly.

After a few sips, she pressed a button on her
comm bracelet and created an electronic floating screen, which was essentially a rectangle
bordered in subtle white light and filled with an
opaque black space ready for drawing, gaming,
vidchats, and more. Cora's screen floated over
her desk showing her game's coding language,
which looked like random symbols made of odd
curves, dots, and lines.

Cora placed gaming glasses over her eyes
and entered a new adventure. Her lab transformed into a small grass clearing surrounded
by a forest. She took a few tentative steps, ver-
ifying that the glasses were synched with her
thoughts. The glasses read upper-level brain
waves and translated them to movement. The
link between the glasses and the wearer's mind
rarely dropped, but it could only work with direct skin contact.

Through the trees, she spotted Brian Farris, one of her regular users. He was Harold's

nephew and a little older than Cora. His eyes were blue gray, and his hair was black. Like Cora, his avatar was his exact scanned image. He played Mystery Adventures for fun and to help her find bugs. At first, she had resisted Brian's help, but he was quite adept at unraveling her puzzles. With time, she had come to rely on him and looked forward to their lunches after a day of creating new trails.

"How long have you been here?" Cora's avatar stepped toward the edge of the grassy clearing.

"Just a few minutes." Brian's avatar ambled out of the forest. "What's the plan today?"

"I was thinking of hiding the treasure behind a waterfall."

Cora's game created dynamic adventures through several terrains found on Earth. Each terrain started with five to ten trails leading to obstacles that required the gamer to use common sense to overcome them. The reward was a treasure needed for the next trail in the game. Cora turned toward a distant mountain range. "Would you do me a favor and play the valley trail again? I made some changes last night, but I wasn't able to check them."

"Up late again?" He turned toward the mountain range. "You realize you just told me where you're going to place the treasure?" He grinned.

"I didn't tell you which waterfall, and I didn't tell you how to get under the water." She raised an eyebrow. "No peeking."

"Wait. Before we get started, how did it go with the family meeting?" he asked.

"About as I expected." She pulled her curly hair behind her head and tied it into a loose bun. "Aunt Ferna wanted Oliver to move in—Harold and I said no. She cried..." She sighed. "I wish he wouldn't get Aunt Ferna so upset. Anyway, it turns out he never intended to live in the family home." She changed to a mocking tone of voice. "He loves Lunar City and doesn't want to leave. He only needs a few credits to tide him over."

"Okay, so nothing new." He surveyed the ground for a moment. "How long before he comes back, do you think?"

"He asks for credits about four times a year. This is October, so he should be back around January," she sighed. "He should be gone by late afternoon."

"Are you okay?" He asked, a serious expression on his face. "I know he likes to use his abilities against you."

"He tried poking me," she said with a note of disgust.

Brian stared with wide eyes.

"It was a mild attack—he's always testing me. I shielded my mind when he arrived last night."

"What about right now? I can pick you up, so you won't have to stay shielded," Brian spoke in a tender voice.

Cora's lips curved with a gentle smile. "Thanks for the offer. I left the house this morning—I'm actually at my computer lab."

Brian grinned. "Of course, my resourceful girl always finds a solution."

Cora blushed, which meant her avatar blushed as well. She turned away. "Um... Let's get started."

"Sure, I'll let you know if I find something." Brian turned away and disappeared into the forest.

Cora strolled in a different direction, heading toward the mountain range in the distance. She stepped into one of the many portals in her game that allowed her to cover expansive terrain in an instant. A moment later, she stood inside a dim cave. She grinned as she surveyed her work that had resulted in a realistic-looking cave.

She got to work creating an old-fashioned treasure box, and using her comm bracelet, filled it with gems and a new map to guide her users to the next treasure. Her users had to unlock every map by answering a common sense science question. This one was about animals that lived in caves. She used her bracelet and created a hole in the floor, inserted the treasure box with the map, and filled the cavity.

Suddenly, Cora jumped, hearing a footstep behind her.

"What're you doing here?" she gasped, finding Steven, one of her players, behind her.

"Sorry. Didn't mean to startle you." As Steven's avatar spoke, he examined the ground beside Cora. He was a pale-faced, thin, thirty-something man she had attended school with over ten years ago. He used an eye implant that rendered a lifelike image of himself as his avatar. Cora and Brian both used Mystery Adventure's resources to render their less accurate avatars. "Is that where you hid the new treasure?"

"Steven, this is supposed to be a surprise," she folded her arms. "I let you join my game as a tester, not a hacker."

Although Steven worked as a programmer testing military code, he sometimes took not-so-legal hacking jobs. Though they had been friends for over ten years, she never felt completely comfortable around him due to his extracurricular activities.

He chuckled. "Alright, okay. Don't get upset." He faced Cora and arranged a more solemn face. "I needed to reach you quickly. If it's any consolation, it took me fifteen minutes to break in here. Your game's defenses are pretty good, and I don't say that to anyone."

"Thanks—I think." She lowered her arms. "Okay, so what do you want?"

Steven shifted from foot to foot. He opened and closed his mouth as if he wanted to start speaking.

"Okay, tell me when you're ready. I have another treasure to create."

She stepped away from him, heading for the next portal.

"Wait, Cora." He sighed. "This will only take a moment. Um... how do you feel?"

"What? How do I feel? What's going on Steven?" She put her hands on her hips, looking a lot like a scolding mom.

He took a step back and glanced about the cave.

"Okay, Steven," she said. "What's really going on? Are you in trouble?"

"Yes... No... Maybe..." He sighed. "I can't say."

"Okay... What do you want me to do?"

"Just answer the question." He spoke in a quiet voice that was so unlike him, it sent a shiver down her spine.

"I'm fine, Steven. Are you okay?" She asked in a low voice.

"Yes, of course. I just..." He huffed. "I need to get going." He pressed his comm bracelet and vanished.

She stared at the spot vacated by Steven for a moment.

"Emma, where's Brian?" she said aloud.

"In field three-A. He's found the treasure map, but he can't open it." Emma replied in an efficient female voice. Emma was Mystery Adventure's AI that assisted Cora's programming, monitored players, scanned for viruses, and more.

Cora turned and entered a portal which took her to Brian, who stood in an enormous field full of wildflowers.

"Having any luck?" she asked with a huge grin as she watched him pacing around a gray and white granite stone about a meter high. A sign floated just over the rock that read 'Time to Step Into the Out.'

"Ugh..." Brian huffed. "I've been working on this ever since I left you. There's no solution!"

She chuckled. "There's definitely a solution, and I'm sure you'll figure it out in a day or two."

"You're a bit smug," he said irritably.

"It takes me days to come up with one puzzle. The least you could do is take one day to figure it out." She grinned. "Anyway, I came to talk to you about Steven."

"Steven? Oh, I remember." He glanced at the granite rock before turning his attention to her. "What's wrong with him?"

"I don't know exactly." Cora furrowed her eyebrows as she took slow, deliberate steps around the meter-high boulder. She checked for coding defects as she arranged her thoughts. "He seemed to want to tell me something, then changed his mind. Or maybe realized he couldn't talk about it."

"Nothing sounds unusual to me." Brian followed her around the boulder. "He always seemed a little unstable."

"Yeah, he's unstable, but not like *that*." She turned to face him. "He asked how I was doing.

Okay, I know it's not strange to ask that, but he was so weird about it."

"I still haven't heard anything odd." He surveyed the stone. "The few times I've run into Steven here, he's been a bit... peculiar."

She huffed. "You're probably right—I'm making too much of this."

"Now that we have that settled, how about lunch?" He hooked an arm around hers and guided her to the nearest portal.

"What time is it?" She glanced at a side panel near the portal entrance. "One already! Can you pick me up?"

They stepped through the portal and emerged on the grassy area where they'd both started the game.

"Of course. I'll be there in about ten minutes." He released her arm. "The Flying Bowl? I feel like soup today."

"I'll see you soon."

He pressed a button on his comm and vanished. A moment later, she did the same.

CHAPTER 3

A couple of hours later, Cora strolled into Harold's office, just a short walk from The Flying Bowl. His office was in the quiet section of downtown Tymal, across from a beautiful park. He managed Lunar and Martian mines for wealthy clients who sometimes needed to reach him for last-minute funding, contract decisions, or mining management advice. The location of the office made him more accessible.

Harold also managed Cora's family's mine, on Ganymede, a moon of Jupiter. The Brimble family had gained the mine only a hundred years ago and renamed it Brimble Mining. Cora's grandfather, the first Askovian in the Brimble family, won the mine while gambling. At first, it required huge mounds of credits to make it operational, but over time, it had turned into a glorious prize. Its high yields of alythium were used to neutralize local gravity, and its precious metals for space flight, making it quite profitable.

"Hey," Cora plopped onto a cushy chair across from Harold's desk. She liked his large, elegant office. Two walls displayed expensive artwork, another featured paneled faux wood, and the final, her favorite, consisted entirely of floor-to-ceiling windows.

Harold sat across from Cora in a larger plush dark-brown chair and selected a few buttons on his comm. "Hello. Something to drink?"

"Water. Just a small cup." She almost sighed with relief—it was such a pleasure to be among family and not have to shield her mind.

He pressed something on his side of the desk that Cora couldn't see. A small cup of water materialized on the table in front of her.

She immediately gulped down half the cup. "Thanks. I guess I was thirstier than I thought."

"More?" he asked.

She shook her head as a screen materialized over the end of his desk to her right.

"What's going on?" she glanced at the empty screen.

Harold leaned back in his chair.

"A few weeks ago, Etta Johanson contacted me. She's related to the Spencer family—you know, one of my clients."

Cora nodded. "She sounds familiar."

"She's a Seer—"

"*That's* why I've heard of her," she interrupted. "Harold, please tell me you don't believe in that hocus pocus."

He chuckled. "No. In fact, I happen to know she's a first-rate con artist—that's why I recorded our conversation." He shifted in his seat as the smile faded from his face. "I've been wondering what to do about it."

"Do? About what?" She took a sip of water.

"I'll explain momentarily." He swiped his hand over the screen. "Watch this first."

The screen showed an older woman in her seventies, fit and trim, with a head full of thick white hair. Her two-piece matching top and bottom clothes were expensive, but dated. She sat across the desk from Harold.

"Hello, Etta. How are Mabel, Alice, and Jessica?" Harold asked, settling back into his chair.

"My cousins are just fine. However, only last week I warned Jessica to be careful of an upcoming negotiation. Of course, she wouldn't listen..." Etta's voice trailed off as she examined something off-screen.

"Do you need credits? I'm not trying to be rude, but it's really the only reason you visit me."

Etta sat straight in her chair and surveyed Harold for a moment. "Last night, I experienced a disturbing vision."

Harold's face twitched as if trying not to smile.

Etta must have noticed, because her chin tilted a notch higher, causing her to look down her nose at Harold.

"I know you don't believe in my Seer abilities, but that doesn't make them less real."

"I'm sorry. What was the vision?" Harold said with a placid face.

Etta examined Harold a moment longer. "Last night, I had a vision. I saw a dark quiet place and a hand pouring powder into a drink. The powder felt evil."

"That sounds terrible."

"Next, I saw you at the Carnation Restaurant. You sat with Sophia, laughing and talking. Four other people sat with you." Etta paused and closed her eyes. "Sorry, I just want to make sure I haven't forgotten anything."

"Of course. Take your time."

"The hand placed the drink with the dissolved powder on a tray. A robot carried the tray to your table and distributed the drinks. That drink with the dissolved powder ended up in front of Sophia." Etta paused again and closed her eyes.

"Was the powder poison?"

"Shhh... Don't interrupt," Etta said in a curt voice. "You stood and made a toast to Sophia's birthday. Everyone else stood, toasting their glasses to Sophia. Everyone took a sip—you know the rest."

"Is it okay to talk now?" Harold asked.

Etta nodded, keeping her eyes closed, as if meditating.

"Do you know who it was?"

"I meditated for an hour on this, but whoever it was doesn't want to be found," Etta spoke in a dreamy voice. "Do you have any more questions?"

"Yes. Can you tell me more about the powder?"

"I meditated on that too, but it never came to me. I think the owner of the hand is obscuring parts of my vision. Maybe another Seer." Etta opened her eyes and her gaze bored into

Harold's. "Be very careful. The person who murdered Sophia is going to kill again."

"Well, that's disturbing news," Harold said while surveying his desk. "Would you be willing to contact the EGS and tell them what you know?"

The EGS, or Earth Global Security, provided the police force for the entire planet, investigating crimes and enforcing laws.

"They'd never believe me." Etta had shifted uncomfortably in her chair. "I meant this vision for you. Be careful. You or someone you love is in danger from this same person."

The recording ended, and the screen went dark.

Cora gazed at Harold. She expected to sense anxiousness or fright. Instead, through her Feeler ability, she perceived a mixture of his transmitted levity and resolve.

"I know. It's extraordinary," Harold said with a small smile. "She's obviously a fake, but our meeting gave me an idea. I always thought that the verdict of suicide wasn't correct for Sophia. I've wanted to look into things but didn't know where to start."

"What? What're you talking about?" Cora sat up in her chair, speaking sharply. "Of course

Sophia ended her life. She was depressed and took something."

Cora didn't mean to react so strongly, but honestly, the months following Sophia's death had been the best in Cora's life. For the first time, she felt comfortable in her own home, made new friends, gotten to know Brian better, and even added players to her game.

Now she knew why Harold had been so preoccupied. He had always treated her like a daughter, unless Sophia was around. Her sister had made him cold and distant. Talk of revisiting Sophia's death seemed to bring her back to life and take away Cora's newfound happiness.

"She's not the type to take her life," Harold said firmly. "Technically, the EGS never found a cause of death. Even though her symptoms were consistent with poisoning, they never found evidence of medication, toxin, or virus. They defaulted to suicide because of her depression, but they never found proof she took the substance or if it was given to her. They should've done more."

She sensed his anger, but she tried to dissuade him again. "There are so many holes in Etta's story, and you just said you believe she's a fraud. Some disembodied hand put an unknown powder in a drink? Something untraceable? How did it end up in front of Sophia instead of someone else?"

"I agree. The EGS can test for hundreds of thousands of poisons, and somehow the coroner couldn't find the poison that killed Sophia?" He settled back in his chair. "Even though I don't believe Etta's vision, I still don't think Sophia ended her life."

"Why do you want to look into Sophia's death if you agree poison isn't likely?" Disbelief laced her voice.

He reached into a drawer and pulled out a bag of pink and yellow sweets. "Do you want one?"

Cora shook her head.

"I know I could be wrong, but I want to make sure I've looked into every possibility. Sophia didn't take her own life." He crunched on a yellow treat and relaxed into his chair.

"Think about this. Someone paid Etta to make that prediction to you. Ask yourself why." She placed her cup back on the table. "I'm afraid you'll trigger the next step of this hoax, and that could be the real danger. I think you should leave this alone, but if you have to go ahead, call the EGS."

"No, no, no." Harold shook his head. "First, I paid Etta from her share of the Spencer mines. She comes around two or three times a year asking for a few credits because she's exceeded her income. I basically give her an advance on her income. Second, we can't afford to have our private business made public."

"She exceeds her income?" She raised her eyebrows. "That means she always needs credits, and someone else could still be paying her. I still think her timing is suspicious—it's so close to the anniversary of Sophia's death."

Harold sighed and popped a pink treat into his mouth.

"Well, at least call the EGS." She leaned forward in her chair. "I'm sure they'll be discreet. Remember that case with the Wilton family a few years ago? Their daughter's—"

"And yet we all know what happened." He shook his head, interrupting Cora. "No, this is a family matter, and that's how it'll stay."

Cora slumped into her chair and gazed out of the window, feeling defeated.

"I haven't told you my plan to use Etta's services," Harold crunched on his sweet. "But I'll need your help to pull it off."

"No, Harold. This is dangerous. Let's call the EGS."

"All you have to do is agree with me when we go to meet the McCarthys in a couple of days," Harold continued, as if she hadn't spoken. "Please come with me."

"No. I'm not going."

She stood.

"Wait, don't go yet." He lumbered to his feet. "Hear me out, and if you still don't want to, you can go."

She hesitated and glanced out the windows. She clasped her hands together to hide her trembling fingers. Going against Harold made her uneasy. After a moment, she retook her seat.

"I want to have a second dinner party at the Carnation in a couple of weeks to commemorate Sophia's birthday."

Sophia was born almost nine years before Cora, and they had shared the same birth month. Sophia's birthday usually overshadowed Cora's, and it seemed like this year would be no different.

"Don't you think it's unusual to celebrate a birthday for someone who's... not around anymore?"

"Yes, yes. Let me think. A commemorative dinner celebrating Sophia's life!" Harold grinned. "I like that better."

She sensed a wave of his excitement mixed with anger and fear. But her mind flashed through the scene a year ago of Sophia laughing and chatting with everyone at her birthday party. Harold had made a toast as everyone lifted their glasses. She watched in slow motion as Sophia gasped and keeled over. Cora shivered.

"With Etta's help, I can flush out the killer," Harold said and formed his mouth into a grim line.

"I don't understand. How will Etta help?"

"Simple. I'll pay her to make another prediction that will rattle the real killer." A small smile lit Harold's face. "I also have a secret second step to help me capture him."

"Him? So you have someone in mind."

"Yes. My first thought is to look at the people closest to Sophia—I mean, the people sitting at the table. There's an endless array of technology that can kill discreetly. I've read about equipment that induces heart attacks, causes seizures, produces aneurysms, and more." He suddenly raised both hands. "I know what you're going to say, 'that's military tech.' But the

McCarthys work for the government and would have indirect access to that tech."

"Harold, I don't think you should go digging up the past." She sighed. The EGS had decided Sophia died by suicide because she had an affair that ended badly. She had left a series of messages declaring she wanted to end it all. The messages hadn't shown the name of the other person. Cora didn't want to bring up any of this for fear of hurting Harold. Instead, she said, "It's not safe. If you really want to go through with this, you have to alert the EGS."

"Hold on... At least take some time and think it over. Will you promise?"

"I'll think it over, but I won't do anything with Etta." She crossed her arms, hoping Harold would give up his crazy plan and go back to being the strong father-figure he'd been to her.

"Thank you. I'll come up with a new plan." He sighed and slouched into his chair. "I just feel that I'm right. Somebody killed her."

Cora sensed the gentle waves of his sadness.

A moment later, Ruby Gibson, Harold's assistant, entered the office. She wore a plain dress, kept her blond hair in a tight bun, and always carried her electronic notepad instead of a comm bracelet.

"Good afternoon, Cora," Ruby said as she stepped into the office.

She glanced at Ruby, but she never sensed Ruby's emotions, which made her an Askovian. Most Askovians worked hard to gather wealth and power. Either the Gibsons weren't interested in wealth and power, or they hadn't figured out how to get it. Ruby's calm demeanor also allowed her to hide her feelings, which would, at the very least, make her an excellent gambler. Cora wondered for the thousandth time why Ruby continued working for Harold.

"Do you know Etta?" Cora asked Ruby.

"Yes, she comes around a few times a year, I believe," Ruby spoke in her typical calm manner.

"I have to find out what happened to my wife," Harold said, his mouth formed a grim line.

"Digging up the past is a bad idea," Cora frowned.

"May I interrupt?" Ruby asked. "I need to handle that issue with Oliver. You said you wanted to look over the message to the Lunar Shuttle Captain, asking him to verify Oliver's arrival on the moon."

"No, it's fine. I trust you," Harold exhaled and suddenly looked much older. Cora perceived his sadness flowing towards her—he still missed Sophia.

"Would you mind sharing your ride?" Ruby asked, addressing Cora. "I'm meeting Oliver at a hotel nearby, then escorting him to the spaceport. You could drop me off first before you go home."

"Wait, I thought he was at the house visiting with his mom?" Cora raised an eyebrow.

"Yes, I know," Harold said. "He told everyone he planned to spend the day with Ferna, but he left the house a couple of hours after us. I think he siphoned a few credits from her. I've sent for the family car. It should be here in a few minutes."

"Are you ready?" Ruby asked.

Cora stood and started for the door.

Ruby followed, but turned back to Harold. "I'll let you know how it goes."

"If he gives you any trouble, call me immediately."

Ruby nodded.

Cora listened to Harold and Ruby, then stepped out of the office.

CHAPTER 4

Twenty minutes later, Cora flopped onto one end of a U-shaped padded sofa in the Brimble's family car, while Ruby sat opposite her. A moment later, it lifted off the ground, and Cora didn't want to appear rude, wracking her brain for something to say. Fortunately, Ruby began first.

"Oh, I meant to ask you, how is your game coming along?" Ruby asked politely, a genuinely inquisitive expression on her face.

"Things are going well."

"When do you think you'll launch it?"

"My target is a year from now." Cora sighed, "I'd hoped it would go faster, but my testers found a lot of bugs."

"Well, that's a good thing. Better now than with paying customers."

"True. Brian keeps telling me I should launch now and get feedback from users."

"That makes sense, too. You could tailor future changes to your customers." Ruby spoke in a gentle voice. "What would you rather do?"

"I'm not sure. I'm still thinking things over," Cora said.

Ruby nodded and then sighed.

"You're not looking forward to dealing with Oliver," Cora said as a statement, not a question.

"Is it that obvious? He's always so difficult."

"What's the plan with him, anyway?"

"I've bought a ticket for him on the last Lunar shuttle today. I'll transfer credits to his account once he boards. Unfortunately, I'll have to babysit him to make sure he *actually* boards." She gathered her electronic pad and small bag. "It looks like we're nearly there."

The car began descending, and Cora glanced through the window and spotted a group of people waiting on the sidewalk.

"Since you've dealt with Oliver before, you're familiar with his Feeler ability," Cora said as she mulled over the last time he'd challenged her. "He can make you feel things that aren't real."

"I can block Feeler abilities," Ruby said with a sigh. "Unfortunately, that means I have to listen to his whining for two hours before his shuttle leaves."

A moment later, the car reached the surface. Even in the car, Cora shielded her mind. Humans without special abilities always broadcast their emotions—they couldn't help it. Askovians with special abilities could shield their feelings, but many chose not to because most of them couldn't sense what other people felt. As a Feeler, she sensed emotions, but too many people made her feel overwhelmed.

Automatically following the traffic, the car drifted to the hotel's entrance. Cora took in the spectacle of Tymal's main street, which contained a mishmash of tall modern buildings used for finance, quaint old-fashioned buildings containing apartments, as well as a varied mix of buildings containing restaurants, art galleries, coffeehouses, and more. She enjoyed observing the hustle and bustle of people crammed onto the sidewalk and darting between floating cars. When her car reached its destination, Cora gazed skyward at a tall exclusive hotel. The car slowed to a stop and Ruby pressed a button near her seat, causing the doors to slide open.

"Hallo Ruby and cousin Coraline," Oliver said with a broad smile.

"Oliver," Ruby said, "Why are you out here?"

"Oh, a bit of nonsense about needing more credits," Oliver said, waving a hand through the air. He turned to Cora. "Aren't you going to give me a hug?"

"No!" Cora exclaimed, and immediately turned pink. She didn't mean to be rude, but after breakfast, she could hardly stand being around Oliver.

Oliver let out a deep, hearty guffaw.

"I think we should let her go." Ruby turned back to Cora with a small smile. "I'll see you tomorrow."

"Goodbye cousin." Oliver waved his fingers and continued to chuckle.

Cora pressed a button near her seat. The car doors closed, and the car lifted into the air. She sighed with relief as she headed home.

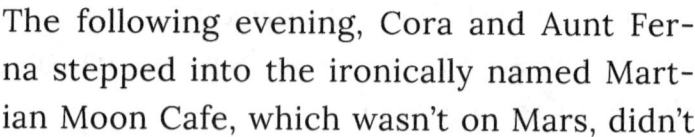

The following evening, Cora and Aunt Ferna stepped into the ironically named Martian Moon Cafe, which wasn't on Mars, didn't have any food from either of its moons, and wasn't a cafe, but a vegan restaurant. Cora chose the popular restaurant out of curiosity, but she didn't expect anything extraordinary. It was considered a high-end restaurant and, as a result, she wore a stylish peach-colored floor-length dress that hugged her waist but flowed around her ankles. Aunt Ferna wore a dark gray pants suit that flowed around her legs and arms.

Cora scanned the restaurant and grinned. "This is fantastic. It feels as if we're at a restaurant in Anteros with a view of the reddish, rocky landscape."

Aunt Ferna giggled. "It does look like Mars. I love it here already. I can't wait to order."

A moment later, a half-meter-high red and black robot floated to them. "Do you have a reservation?"

"Yes, it's under Ferna Robertson," her aunt replied.

"Please follow me." The red and black robot turned and floated away, following a curved aisle.

Cora followed while gazing at the windows. "I read that the vid feed is live from Anteros."

"Was that a meteor?" Aunt Ferna asked, while gazing at the streak of light across the night sky.

"I think so. They're not as common as you might think."

Cora followed the robot to a table and took her seat.

"Oh look, a shuttle is taking off in the distance," Aunt Ferna pointed like an excited child from her chair.

"It must be fantastic just to watch the vids all day." Cora continued gawking at the shuttle until it disappeared.

"Happy thirtieth birthday, my dear," Aunt Ferna said with a broad grin as they tore their gaze away from the windows.

Cora chuckled. "How long have we been doing this?"

"Since you were ten," Aunt Ferna chortled. "It's your special day."

"It smells amazing in here." Cora selected a button on the table and a floating screen containing a menu appeared over the table in front of her. "Oh, I know what I want. Pesto Pasta. They grow a lot of the ingredients in Martian soil, including the pine nuts, basil leaves, and arugula that go into the pasta sauce. The restaurant also seasons the heirloom tomatoes in salts from an ancient Martian sea."

"I think Martian food tastes so much better than Earth's. Don't you?" Aunt Ferna asked.

"Aunt, it's still food from Earth. All they do is mix a little Martian soil with farmland." Cora folded her arms and leaned on the table. "Anyway, what are you going to order?"

"I want the vegan pot pie." Aunt Ferna shivered with excitement. "It has a fluffy pastry top made with Earth flour, but inside is a creamy mix of spring vegetables that've all grown in Martian soil." She grinned. "I can't wait."

They each placed their orders on the menu. Shortly after, a green and white robot floated to the table to deliver their spicy white wine, which was fermented with a mix of grapes and a secret spice.

"Mm…" Aunt Ferna took a second sip. "That's good. What do you think the secret spice is?"

"Don't know, but it's good." She inhaled and felt her muscles relax as she exhaled.

"What's going on with you?" Aunt Ferna took a sip of wine. "We haven't had much time to just sit and talk lately."

"Everything's fine." *Except Harold wants to find Sophia's murderer, and he's come up with a dangerous plan*, Cora thought. But she didn't want to talk about Harold. "Actually, Brian wants me to make plans to release my game. He thinks I should get additional players so that I have more feedback, and he wants me to pick a release date."

"That all sounds reasonable." Aunt Ferna surveyed her. "Why don't you like his plan?"

"Mystery Adventures is my baby. I've nurtured it from infancy. I can't let just anyone play it before it's ready." Cora sighed.

Aunt Ferna chuckled. "Having raised an actual child, I understand." She took a sip of wine. "What do you want for your game?"

"I don't know." Cora examined her wine. "I want to have customers and really create a business, but I just don't feel ready yet."

"Are you sure you're ever going to be ready?" Aunt Ferna said. "Maybe Brian has the right idea. You've been coding for years—you may just need to jump in and see how things work out."

"There are still a lot of bugs to fix." Cora shifted in her seat to watch a shuttle landing.

"My dear, I know little about programming, but games always seem to have bugs. Somehow the bugs are fixed, and later new ones crop up."

Aunt Ferna took a sip of wine. "At some point, you just have to move ahead and launch."

Cora grinned. "I can't argue with your logic." She glanced out of the windows. "Today is my birthday, and I just want to have fun. I'll think about this later."

"Of course, dear." Aunt Ferna's face brightened. "Oliver said you saw him off yesterday."

"Not really. I dropped Ruby downtown—she saw him off," she said.

"I still don't think Harold had a right to cut off Oliver's funds. Oliver wouldn't be in half as much trouble if Harold would simply restore his income from the mine." Aunt Ferna huffed.

Cora wilted as a heaviness settled on her shoulders. *Oliver's continuous gambling would end with selling Brimble mine*, she thought.

"What's the matter?" Aunt Ferna asked.

She didn't want to discuss Oliver. "I guess talking about Oliver made me think of Sophia."

"I know you always felt her birthday overshadowed yours."

"If I'd been stronger, my parents wouldn't have sent me away." Cora's mind flashed to a sunny day when she had been five and Sophia fourteen. Cora had burst into the sunroom and spied her mom and Sophia. "Mom, Mom! Guess what I saw in the garden?" She slowed her steps and eventually had stopped as she felt waves of Sophia's rage crash toward her. The waves of fury and hatred washed over her, filling her mind. She drowned in an ocean of bitterness and pain as her world went black. A few weeks later, her parents had packed her off to a boarding school, explaining it was for her protection, but it had always felt like a punishment.

"When your parents sent you away, you'd done nothing wrong" Aunt Ferna sighed. "They just didn't know what to do about a very headstrong and powerful Askovian, Sophia. They needed to keep you safe from her, and they needed to keep Sophia safe from the EGS who still lock up disruptive uncontrollable Askovians."

Cora pondered for a moment. "I haven't heard of the EGS locking anyone up in years."

"True, it's not as frequent now as it was a few decades ago, but when you and Sophia were children, it was quite common."

The green and white robot floated to their table, interrupting their conversation to deliver their meals.

"Smells amazing." Cora took a bite of her pesto pasta with simulated cheese sprinkled on top. "Tastes divine. I've never had pesto pasta this good."

"Mmm... This is delicious," Aunt Ferna said, taking a second bite of her vegan pot pie. "The pastry is so light and crispy."

The table grew silent for a few minutes while they ate and sipped their wine.

Cora leaned back in her chair. "I think I'm already full."

Aunt Ferna chortled. "Me too. It was delightful." She took another sip of wine. "Will you have room for dessert?"

Cora shook her head and rubbed her stomach. "I don't think so." She glanced around at the other patrons, each dressed in the latest fashions and enjoying their meals. She sighed, reflecting on their previous conversation. "The thing is, mom and dad rarely visited me."

"Well, I didn't say they were perfect." She reached across the table and squeezed Cora's hand.

"I see. They assumed at boarding school I'd be safe, but they forgot I needed my family. Never mind." She shook her head and forced a smile. "This is a happy day. It's my birthday, and I've changed my mind—I want dessert."

"You're right!" Aunt Ferna said with a small smile. "Chocolate?"

"Of course. Let's pull up the menu." Cora's mouth transformed into a grin as her eyes slid over each dessert. "Martian chocolate cake for me. The cacao plants grew in Martian soil. I bet it's good."

"I'll have the Chocolate mousse." Aunt Ferna grinned.

In just a few minutes, the green and white robot appeared at the table with their desserts and two cups of coffee.

"Despite our conversation, I hope you've had a decent birthday." Aunt Ferna sipped her coffee.

"Decent, no. It was fantastic. But I still think this Martian soil stuff is a gimmick." Cora chuckled. "It doesn't change the fact that the food is delicious. I would love to come here again."

CHAPTER 5

Cora woke late the next morning, and with Oliver gone, felt as if her life had returned to normal. Contentment settled in her chest as her eyes opened to greet the day.

"Haley, lights," Cora said, speaking to the home's AI. A second later, the lighting in her room increased. She glanced at the shading over her windows. "Haley, open the shades." Sunlight flooded her room as she rolled to her side, grabbed her comm bracelet on her bedside table, and stood.

Pacing to her window, she surveyed her home's back garden and grinned. She loved meandering along the trails, weaving around the fountain, flowers, and trees.

She selected a button on her bracelet. A moment later, coffee, synthetic eggs, and sausage appeared from the meal crafter on the small dining table in her room. Wolfing down her breakfast, she sipped on her coffee when her bracelet chimed. She waved her hand over the bracelet, and Harold's image hovered over her desk.

"Good morning," Harold said with a broad smile. "Did you sleep well?"

"Yes. You?" Cora took a sip of coffee.

"Fine... I may have a safer way to execute my plan." He leaned forward. "I'm scratching Etta—she's a fraud, anyway. Instead, I'll have the commemorative dinner at the Carnation Restaurant and invite everyone who attended last year."

"What about your plan to trap the killer?"

"Yesterday, I realized the second part of my plan will work just fine without her." He chuckled.

"What's the second part of your plan?"

"I'm going to record everything at the party." He grinned. "I don't just mean surveillance video, but heart rate, blood pressure, brain waves,... all biometric data."

"You can't use those biometric recordings without permission."

"Oh, that doesn't matter," he said with a wave of his hand. "I'm just trying to get the EGS to look in a new direction. They'll still need to gather their own evidence." He surveyed Cora for a moment. "Now you have to admit, this plan is completely safe. The killer will never know, and we only have to behave the way we normally would."

"So, during the commemorative dinner, someone will mention Sophia and probably have a toast to her, or maybe a speech." She shifted in her chair with her eyebrows furrowed. "A killer with a conscience would become uncomfortable, showing unusual bio readings. If there was no killer, which I think is the case, there should be no peculiar reactions."

"Exactly!" He rubbed his hands together.

"However, a killer with no conscience also won't have any suspicious responses," Cora said. "Your plan doesn't cover all situations."

"I know, but it's the best I've got right now." He sighed. "Have you mulled things over? Will you come with me to the McCarthys and Tristan Quimby to persuade them to come to the dinner?"

"Before I agree, let me look into Etta." She furrowed her eyebrows. "Something's off about her."

"When you say, 'look into', what do you mean, exactly?" He gazed at her. "I can't have you upsetting the Spencers.

"I'll be discreet. Actually, I'm not interested in the Spencers at all," Cora said. "Give me the morning to look into Etta. I'll let you know in a couple of hours."

"Good, good..." He paused. "How about, if I don't hear from you by twelve, I'll go on my own?"

"Harold, this is..." She sighed. "It's just so unlike you to be reckless. You'd have used Etta if I hadn't refused. Now you're sprinting into your plan to recreate Sophia's dinner. If there really is a killer, you'll be in danger."

"I don't see it that way." He leaned into the screen. "I see it as my duty to bring Sophia's killer to justice. I just can't rest until I do everything in my power to make that happen."

"Okay. I'll call you in a couple of hours." She drooped into her chair as her morning happiness evaporated. She wished she could get out of going, but Harold could get into some serious trouble if she didn't get involved.

Cora opened a new floating screen and connected to the Net. "Alright Etta, who hired you?" She started with a general search for Etta Johanson and discovered very little information. "Hmm... Etta at the Briny Club." She sipped her coffee and mumbled to herself. "What're you doing at an Askovian private club? Something's missing. Haley message Brian for a vidchat."

A few minutes later, Cora heard a chime. "Incoming from Brian," Haley said. "Shall I put him through?"

"Yeah," Cora said and gulped the last of her coffee as the vidchat began and Brian's image appeared over her desk.

"Hey. How's it going?" Brian asked as he munched on something round and crunchy.

"Are those choco puffs?" Cora asked, completely distracted by the loud sound.

He said something with a full mouth, but she couldn't understand.

"Okay, never mind," she said. "Would you put that down? I need to talk to you."

"Fine," he said, as he put his food aside. "What's going on?"

"I need information about Etta Johanson," she said. "So far, I've done a simple Net search and found her mentioned at the Briny Club, and not in a good way. What's strange is she doesn't show up anywhere else. It's almost as if she doesn't exist."

"I don't suppose you can tell me why you're looking up Etta Johanson?"

"Have you noticed that Harold's been distracted for the past few weeks?"

"Yeah. I just assumed he was... mourning." He cleared his throat and reached for a cup of water.

"Etta told him about her Seer vision."

"Are you serious?" Brian snickered, interrupting Cora.

"Unfortunately, yes. Harold knows she's a fraud, but she's a cousin of the Spencer family. He doesn't want to step on any toes."

"Okay, well, since she's a fraud, just ignore anything she says." He eyed his bag of choco puffs.

"She told Harold about a vision where a disembodied hand murdered Sophia by pouring poison into her cup." She smirked. "The whole thing is ridiculous."

"I thought there wasn't any evidence of poisoning?" He popped a choco puff in his mouth and hurried to chew and swallow.

"There's no evidence." She leaned forward. "What I want to know is who paid her?"

"Didn't Uncle Harold give her an advance from her income? Many Askov family members can't live within their means."

"Well, yes. But she just showed up out of the blue." She raised her hands, exasperated.

"The little I've heard of Etta is that she makes the rounds." Brian shifted his bag from one side of the desk to the other. "She floats between relatives and friends, asking for 'just a few credits.' I think she was just low on credits."

Cora grimaced. "I suppose that makes sense."

"Etta isn't wealthy, but the Spencers are. I'm sure they pay to keep her information off the Net." Brian popped a small choco puff in his mouth.

"The thing is, she's scammed a couple of people at the Briny Club with her Seer act," she said while reaching for her empty cup.

"I wonder if that was an oversight by the Spencer family," he said. "They removed her from the global Net, but not the Briny Club internal network."

"No, not an oversight. Even though it's an old club, they have world-class security. It's difficult to tamper with their internal network and remove information." She scratched her head. "The thing is, the Spencer sisters, Mabel, Alice, and Jessica, are all on the Net. Of course, only good things, but nothing about Etta. I can't find where she lives, works, or anything."

"You could just ask the Spencers," he said, crunching on another puff.

"I thought of that." She frowned. "I just don't know when I'll see them, and I don't want to make it a big deal by arranging a special appointment."

"Based on what I've heard, she's harmless." He shifted in his chair. "Except for being a fraud."

"She's not that harmless—she's left a wake of disgruntled people." Her eyebrows furrowed in thought. "Well, it seems Harold won't use her anyway, but something about her isn't right."

"Sorry, I couldn't help more."

"It's okay." Cora sipped her coffee and gazed out the window at the garden.

"Something's bothering you." Brian put away his choco puffs. "I'm a great listener."

"I know you are," she said and smiled. "Harold wants us to go to the McCarthys this afternoon to invite them to a commemorative dinner for Sophia. It's at the Carnation. I would love to say no, but Harold's so set on this dinner."

"*That* restaurant..."

"I know. I think it's such a bad idea, but he won't listen," she said.

"Okay. What's the worst that could happen if you said no?"

"Harold's not really himself right now," she said. "He could get into some serious trouble."

"I don't think too much could happen in a crowded restaurant."

She frowned. "I suppose it'll be okay."

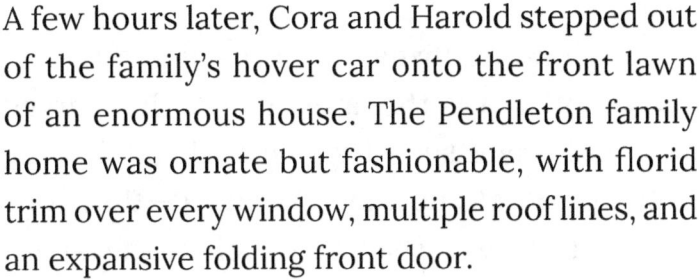

A few hours later, Cora and Harold stepped out of the family's hover car onto the front lawn of an enormous house. The Pendleton family home was ornate but fashionable, with florid trim over every window, multiple roof lines, and an expansive folding front door.

In most Askov families like the Pendletons, only a few members possessed special abilities, while the other family members took positions in government or controlled large corporations. Regardless, the entire family became known as an Askov family.

Cora and Harold strolled to the folding front door, and she spied more of the elaborate trim surrounding the entrance. Shielding herself from other people's emotions always left her feeling a little blind to the world. Her stomach tightened as she anticipated an uncomfortable meeting.

Harold waved a hand over the small glass square to the right of the door. A moment later, one panel of the folding door opened and a small robot around a meter high stood in the doorway.

"Good afternoon, Harold Albright," the robot said. "I'm Gilly. Who, may I ask, is accompanying you?"

"I'm Coraline Brimble," Cora said, gazing at the robot. It was the latest model that served as a butler and security guard. These tiny robots were not to be underestimated—they contained an array of weapons to defend the family. They also maintained an extensive library of safe people to allow inside. She wondered if her name was on the accepted list.

A moment later, Gilly glided into the house. "Please follow me." They trailed behind Gilly as she navigated a short hallway and entered a formal sitting room.

"Harold and Coraline," Councilor Vivian McCarthy said, stepping forward to shake hands.

She dressed in an expensive pale lavender dress, perfect for casual business meetings. Her piercing blue eyes suggested a keen and clever mind. She worked as a diplomat to the Lunar City Council, acting as the face of the Pendleton political arm.

"Harold!" Professor Wesley McCarthy said from where he stood near an antigrav cart that floated at waist height and offered an assortment of containers with drinks. He was tall and striking, but not a pretty-boy, like cousin Oliver. He taught archeology at a prestigious university. He smiled at Harold, but it didn't reach his cold blue eyes. "Would you like a drink?"

"No, thank you Wesley," Harold said, turning to him.

"Coraline?" Wesley asked and held a container of a dull orange liquid.

She shook her head. "No, thank you."

Vivian waved her arm toward a sofa. "Please, have a seat."

Cora and Harold settled on the pale sage sofa and glanced around the sitting room. It was very traditional, but still in line with the latest fashion, and significantly more ornate than she would've liked. It reminded her of her mother's decorating style with ornate sofa cushions and chairs, pale flowery drapes that reached the floor, and bookcases with real books. Physical books were very expensive, and she wondered if they read them, or they were part of the decor. She noticed their home's design placed all modern electronics out of sight, and even the robot Gilly disappeared once Harold and Cora entered the sitting room.

Wesley and Vivian sat opposite the sofa, each in their own cushioned chair. The furniture's arrangement, stiff and formal, suited a room for discussing policy and deciding the fate of the world. She imagined they had a more inviting room for family and friends.

"Coraline, I haven't seen you for a while," Wesley said, reclining in his chair. "How've you been?"

"Just fine," Cora said and paused, scrambling for something to add. "I've been working on my game. It's an educational puzzle game."

"That sounds interesting." Vivian took a sip of a pale pink drink. "What kinds of puzzles?"

"Players need to use math and science to solve them. I'm trying to make it common sense math and science so everyone can enjoy it."

"Oh, I'd be interested in trying it out." Vivian's face lit up. "I have a degree in engineering, though I've never used it."

"I'd be terrible at it," Wesley chuckled. "I prefer ancient history."

"Well, she did say common sense. It's meant for everybody." Vivian turned to Wesley as she spoke.

"So, what brings you two here?" Wesley said, redirecting the conversation as he took a sip of an amber-colored drink.

"I plan to host a commemorative dinner celebrating Sophia's life." Harold turned from Wesley to Vivian. "It's at the Carnation, and I want everyone who was there a year ago to attend."

"I can't make it," Wesley said right away.

"I haven't even told you any dates," Harold said softly.

"What Wesley *means* to say is he's in the middle of an archeology lecture series, and I'm involved with a series of meetings between Earth Global Nations and the Lunar City Council," Vivian said with a placating smile. "We're not available for social engagements at this time."

"Are you also busy on weekends?" Harold asked in a low voice.

Cora recognized this tactic. The quieter Harold spoke, the more others negotiating with him had to focus and listen to his words. It would have the effect of moving negotiations along more quickly as he replied with solutions to each of their excuses.

"This coming weekend is completely full," Wesley said and crossed his arms.

"I was thinking of two or three weeks from now," Harold said calmly.

Wesley scowled. "Well, I... Check with my AI, she'll let you know when I'm free." Wesley stumbled over his words and gulped the last of his drink.

Cora raised both eyebrows. She hadn't expected such strong resistance from Wesley.

"Let's call her now. What's her name?" Harold asked with a small smile.

Vivian chuckled, "Let's make this easier for everyone." She selected a button on her comm bracelet and a private screen appeared, hovering over her bracelet. Cora couldn't see any contents on the screen, but Vivian used her fingers to sift through data. "Here we are. How about in ten days on a Saturday? Does that work for you, Harold?"

Vivian is taking this so lightly. She must know Harold's negotiation tactics, she thought.

"Thank you so much, Vivian," Harold beamed at her.

Wesley flashed a scowl at his wife before plastering a smile on his face. "Yes, I hope that date works for your commemorative dinner."

"I know this is an inconvenience for you, but I really appreciate you attending dinner. It'll be our send-off for Sophia."

"Wesley and I would be honored to attend your dinner," Vivian said with a broad smile.

Wesley nodded but said nothing as he studied Harold for a moment, and an awkward silence followed.

"Well, I don't want to take up too much of your time," Harold said. "I think we should return home."

Cora surveyed Wesley. Her curiosity overtook her common sense, and she lowered her shield for a moment, focusing on Wesley. Unexpectedly, a tsunami of Vivian's anger, resentment, and fear washed over and nearly drowned her because of its intensity.

The room twisted, and she stretched out her hands, trying to steady herself. She raised her shield and breathed a sigh of relief, but the room continued to spin.

Harold grasped her hand. "Are you alright Cora?" He placed her second hand on her arm. "Should I get a medipad?"

The thought of a medipad, an automated floating medical unit that handles first aid injuries, made Cora's face burn with embarrassment. The image of a floating robot scanning and probing her while everyone stared flashed through her mind and made her want to crawl into a hole.

"No, no. I'm fine... I just had a dizzy spell." She tried to smile at Wesley and Vivian. "I'm sorry to trouble you." She stumbled to her feet. "Harold, I think I'd better get home."

"If you're sure. We can borrow the McCarthys' medipad if you need it." Harold's eyebrows knitted with concern.

Her mind flashed through a series of memories of Sophia's and Oliver's relentless teasing as they called her weak. The room stopped spinning, and she forced a confident smile. "I'm fine. Come, Harold." Cora took a couple of steps away from the sofa. "Thank you for meeting with us," she addressed the McCarthys, and they left the house.

CHAPTER 6

"I heard from Oliver today," Aunt Ferna told the table at lunch the next day. Cora glanced up at Harold across from her, who kept his eyes on his plate.

Ferna dusted a crumb off her striped pastel dress and hummed as she helped herself to a second serving of lunch from the meal crafter.

Cora glanced down at her own dress, with its cheerful floral print that made it suitable for both casual and formal occasions, and noted that the bright dress didn't match her mood. She was poking at her lunch, brooding over her last conversation with Brian. *Maybe she should tell Harold she won't help him any longer. What's the worst that could happen?* she thought.

Harold's mind also seemed far away; dressed in a formal, tailored, black jumpsuit, he ate in fits and starts.

Cora sensed Aunt Ferna's radiated cheerfulness, which contrasted with Harold's broadcast sadness. She wished for the thousandth time she could help Harold feel at peace about Sophia's passing.

"He's doing well in Lunar City, and he's thinking of coming home for New Year's," Aunt Ferna said and grinned.

Cora stifled a groan—she knew Oliver had no intention of visiting for the New Year's celebration. He just liked to play with his mom's emotions. But she loved her aunt and didn't want to say anything to hurt her feelings. She simply said, "How does Oliver like his new job?"

"He didn't say much. Just that everything's going well," Aunt Ferna said with a bright smile. "I thought perhaps we should start planning for the New Year's celebrations." She popped a bite into her mouth, chewed, and swallowed. "I want to have a party here, like we used to when Sophia and your mother were with us. We have the space, and if we start now, we can hire a good caterer."

"It's hard to think about parties right now," Cora said. "Can't we do it next year?"

"There's never enough time to plan a party, but plenty of time to enjoy it," Aunt Ferna said.

"In any case, dear, I think you and Harold need something to take your mind off things."

Harold snapped out of his reverie and blinked at Aunt Ferna. "What—What's that? A party? When?"

"New Year's Eve party," Aunt Ferna shook her head. "Haven't you been listening?"

"Sorry, Ferna," Harold said, sitting straighter in his chair. "I think a New Year's Eve party is a good idea. We used to have them when I first married Sophia." Harold's face clouded, but he forced a smile. "It'll give us all something to look forward to."

"Excellent! I'll start looking for caterers," Aunt Ferna said with a broad smile. "I wonder if Markey's Catering is still in business. We haven't used them for a few years."

"Yes, well, we should be going," Harold glanced at Cora.

"Of course, the commemorative dinner." Cora glanced at Harold—this was her last chance to back out.

"What? What dinner?" Aunt Ferna asked.

Harold sighed and frowned at Cora. "I meant to tell you later." He addressed Aunt Ferna. "I want to have a commemorative party celebrating Sophia's life. I've invited the McCarthys and now that Cora has inherited Sophia's mine, she needs to make contacts in the right places."

Most Askov families maintained their wealth with a series of interplanetary mines. The most profitable mined alythium, which alters local gravity. The Brimble family only owned one mine, making it a valuable target. Other Askovians interested in increasing their wealth would attempt to take over a lone mine instead of going after a giant corporation. As the owner, Cora needed to maintain close relationships with larger, more powerful Askov families to keep her mine in the Brimble family.

"Well, that's a wonderful idea, Harold," Aunt Ferna said as she rubbed her hands together. "I love planning parties."

"Actually, I've planned a dinner at Carnation Restaurant." Harold squared his shoulders.

"Oh... But that's where Sophia..." Aunt Ferna said. "Wouldn't it be better to go to a place without bad memories?"

"No, I want to replace those memories with good ones," Harold said and stood. "I hope you can join us."

He didn't wait for her reply. He simply turned on his heel and left the dining room.

"Oh, Cora," Aunt Ferna said as a shadow crossed her face. "You have to talk him out of it. I don't want to go where Sophia—"

"I know, I know," Cora said, and gulped down the last of her coffee. "He's determined, but I'll keep trying to talk him out of it."

"But why would he want to go back there?" Aunt Ferna asked with a worried frown.

Just then, Harold leaned back into the room with a scowl. "Cora, I'm sorry to rush you, but I have another meeting this afternoon."

Cora forced a smile and kissed her aunt on the cheek. "It's alright. I'll talk to Harold," she whispered before turning to follow Harold out of the room.

"Okay, Harold," Cora said as the door to the hover car closed with a whoosh behind her. "Where're we going?"

The car lifted off the ground and headed toward downtown Tymal.

"My Club," Harold said. "I want to invite the last person who attended Sophia's party." He glanced at Cora's clothing. "It's why I asked you to dress up."

She grunted. "I really dislike the Briny Club."

"Cora..." He paused as he gathered his thoughts. "I forgot you had an unpleasant experience there. Fifteen years is a long time, and those kids have either matured or moved on."

"Sophia set those kids on me." Cora surveyed the Krega mountains in the distance.

"She could be a little insensitive," he said in a quiet voice. "I don't think she realized how her behavior hurt others."

"Insensitive? She could be downright *cruel*. She put those kids up to dumping green juice on me. Thank goodness I'm nothing like her."

He sighed and slouched into his seat.

"I know you think this dinner is a bad idea. But that EGS report of suicide has always bothered me." He spoke in a sad, quiet voice. "Imagine a murderer among us, someone we know, and talk to every day. We just can't let them get away with it." He suddenly gripped her arm. "Cora, please help me. Please help me find Sophia's killer."

Cora didn't shield herself around Harold, and so she received the full force of his desperation, sadness, and despair from the contact. Cora felt his rising tide of emotions threatening to engulf her. Panicked, she pulled her arm out of Harold's grip. "I've already agreed to help."

They didn't speak for the rest of the trip, and ten minutes later, the car landed on a pad at the top of a long, flat, fourteen-story building. Cora shielded her emotions as soon as the car touched the roof. She didn't want to become overwhelmed by anyone else's emotions.

The sign in front of their car read, "Briny Highland Club." The club's name came from the numerous salty patches found in the Krega mountains, which used to rest on the ocean floor millions of years ago. They stepped out of the car and headed to the rooftop entrance.

Two men leaving the club and dressed in formal jumpsuits passed by and nodded at Harold but ignored her. A feeling of foreboding settled on her shoulders, even though she had every right to be there. Her grandfather had been a member of this club. Many politicians and wealthy business owners became members in order to influence government policies. Hers and Harold's family business involved mining on Mars and one of Jupiter's moons.

They stepped into the antigrav lift, which moved using the mineral alythium to manipulate gravity and move the elevator up and down. The antigrav lift whisked them from the roof to the first floor. A moment later, the door opened to a serene lobby that featured a formal, elegant desk with a concierge and a row of one-meter-high robots ready to assist anyone staying at the Club or simply eating lunch.

The other end of the lobby featured the entrance to a restaurant and bar. Cora and Harold stepped out and stood near the bank of lifts. The lobby featured artwork from Lunar City, and much of the decor matched it. She wrinkled her nose, not caring for the lonely, desolate landscape outside of Lunar City.

"Tristan. Good to see you," Harold said with a smile as he stepped forward and shook hands with a thirty-something, slender, red-headed man, also dressed in the familiar tailored black jumpsuit. His unfocused blue-green eyes caused him to swing his head while he walked with a slight tilt.

Is he drunk? Cora thought. *It's still early in the day.*

"Harold. It's been a while," Tristan said with a grin. "Looks like I got here right on time." He turned toward Cora. "And who's this lovely flower?"

"My sister-in-law, Cora." Harold turned towards her with a gentle smile.

"Ah yes, Sophia's little sister," Tristan said, as his eyes roamed over every inch of Cora's body.

Cora stifled a shiver and forced a smile—she'd always found him a little creepy, and he wasn't doing anything to change that impression now. She regarded Tristan, now swaying, as one of Sophia's worshipers. She nodded her greeting.

"Cora dear," Tristan stepped closer to her. "What do you think of this artwork?"

Cora surveyed the walls again, trying to think of something positive to say.

"You hate it!" Tristan guffawed. "Thought so. I remembered you as a quiet, intelligent girl with far better taste than her sister."

"I didn't say that," she said.

Cora observed him with a wary expression. Even though he couldn't influence her with Askovian abilities, he could manipulate her with flattery, by lying, or any number of tactics used by normal people.

"Well, I hate it, too." Tristan scanned the room. "I've been to the Lunar landscape dozens of times. I could've rendered something much more interesting." He spoke in a loud voice.

"Tristan, I think we're attracting attention," Harold said, with a gentle tug of Tristan's arm. Harold guided him toward the dining room. "I think we should order some food for you."

Tristan guffawed a second time and more heads turned their way.

Cora rushed after Harold and Tristan as they headed to the dining room. Once she stepped inside, a small, delightful smile spread across her face. The room's decorations were nothing like those of the stuffy lobby. This dining room was light, with a full wall of floor-to-ceiling windows providing a view of Tymal's quaint downtown. She watched passersby darting into stores and stepping out of boutiques with neatly tied packages. Robots easily dodged pedestrians as floating cars drifted overhead. The scene made her want to move downtown, but then she suddenly remembered the people... Too many emotions.

"Cora," Harold called. "Over here." He gestured with an arm wave.

Unlike the eateries she usually frequented with Brian, the Briny Club's restaurant used robots instead of meal crafters. Cora took her seat just as a robot glided to the table. Cora and Harold just ordered fizzy drinks, but Tristan ordered a full lunch. A moment later, the drinks and food arrived. Tristan ate like he'd missed a few meals. Judging by his slim form, that may have been true. After Tristan commented on the Lunar art, she remembered his artwork. She didn't think he worked at a steady job. Maybe Sophia subsidized his work.

"Sorry, I missed breakfast," Tristan said as he scraped the last of his food off his plate. "Now, what did you want to talk about?"

Harold spun the same story he'd used on the McCarthys. He mentioned Sophia's commemorative dinner party and how he desired to share it with everyone who attended the previous one.

"Well, I suppose I could attend, but don't you think it's a little morbid?" Tristan grimaced.

"I view it as a beautiful send-off for my beloved wife." Harold's face drooped as he glanced at the table.

"Of course, I'd be happy to attend," Tristan said in an unexpectedly sober voice. "Just let me know when and where."

"As to that, I've booked the Carnation Restaurant in nine days." Harold sipped his drink.

"The Carnation..." Tristan said with a frown. "But that's where..." He shook his head. "No sorry, I can't do it. That's too much."

Cora hid a smile, hoping Tristan would continue to resist. That might make Harold give up the whole idea.

"I want to replace the events of last year with happy memories," Harold said soberly, lowering his voice. "This is the perfect party to do that."

Cora had seen Harold use this tactic just yesterday. Tristan was doomed.

"I don't..." Tristan started and scratched his head, thinking. "I'll tell you what. Sophia promised to purchase some of the paintings that I have." He simpered. "Would you be interested?"

"I'll look them over after the dinner party and purchase them. You have my word."

"How about a down payment? Say... one hundred credits?"

Cora gasped. Harold had to refuse being blackmailed.

Harold clicked a button on his bracelet. "I can give you fifty credits right now."

"No, I really think one hundred credits is fair," Tristan said with a smirk.

"Cora, let's go," Harold said while he stood.

Cora didn't leave her seat. She'd seen Harold negotiate before—he almost always won, and she knew what he was doing.

"Okay, I'm sorry..." Tristan said, pulling Harold's arm. "Fifty credits is a good amount."

Harold sat again and swiped a hand over his bracelet, sending the fifty credits to Tristan.

"Do you have any questions about meeting at the Carnation?" Harold asked sternly.

"Harold, don't be angry," Tristan's face lightened with a small smile. "I just needed something to tide me over until I sell more art."

"I don't like being manipulated," Harold said with a grim expression.

Cora coughed—she couldn't believe Harold's nerve.

"And what the hell do you think you were doing?" Tristan said with a snicker. "I think we're even."

Cora hid a smile.

"Well..." Harold turned to Cora. "Are you ready to leave?"

"Sure." Cora stood with Harold. She turned to Tristan. "I'll see you in a few days."

A few moments later, Cora and Harold sat in their car, heading home. Cora sighed with relief as she dropped her shield. Though, dropping it made her vulnerable to Harold's tumultuous emotions, which swung from anger to anxiety and sadness to despair. She considered raising her shield again but decided to talk instead.

"Harold, what're you thinking?" Cora asked gently.

"N-Nothing..." Harold snapped his head toward her. "Well... sometimes I wonder if I should just leave things alone. The EGS is happy with death by suicide. I'm the only one..."

"You're not the only one, Harold," Cora said as she squeezed his hand. "If you think there's a real chance someone murdered her, I'll help you." Cora hesitated as she shifted in her seat. "But if someone murdered Sophia, what'd be the motive?"

"Don't know... She had a lot of friends and went to a lot of parties. Maybe she discovered something. Something really incriminating."

"You're thinking of the McCarthys. They're the type to know state secrets, but it'd also be easy for them to discredit Sophia."

"Well, I—"

Cora interrupted him. "Just a minute. Who was Sophia, anyway? I mean, compared to the McCarthys. A social butterfly with artist connections. Who're the McCarthys? Vivian is a diplomat with powerful connections here on Earth and in Lunar City. Even Wesley has ties to most Askov families through his archaeological funding."

"Yes, but—"

Cora cut him off again. "The McCarthys had no reason to be afraid of Sophia," Cora said.

Harold deflated and sagged against the side of the car. "I know you're right, but I don't know what else to do."

Cora felt Harold's broadcast despair, and she couldn't leave him in so much pain. *If I make Harold see that Sophia ended her life, he'll go back to himself, and I'll get my family back,* she thought.

"I still think Sophia took her own life," Cora said. "But the EGS never found the substance that killed her, which means there are some holes in the EGS's suicide theory. I promise I'll keep looking into Sophia's death and find out exactly what happened to her."

Harold nodded. "Thank you."

Cora wondered how she'd keep this promise.

CHAPTER 7

Two days later, Cora stood in a storage room near the back of her house, with piles of formal dresses, shoes, bags, and hats surrounding her. Aunt Ferna asked her to look for clothes suitable for donations to Martian residents in need.

Aunt Ferna and many other people living on Earth relied on Inter-Planetary News (known as IPN) to keep track of loved ones residing in Lunar City on the moon, Anteros on Mars, and many interplanetary outposts.

As interest increased, the IPN produced sensationalized news stories to keep their viewers. Aunt Ferna had seen an often-run news story where a woman cried and begged for those on Earth to send clothing. An explosion in a refinery on Mars had destroyed a small town just outside of the capital, Anteros, and so here was Cora, looking for clothes.

Cora found the news story suspect. Why wasn't the woman asking for food? Why couldn't the woman use the crafters in Anteros for clothing? If the crafters provide enough food for everyone, they should also provide clothing.

She surveyed Sophia's old clothes, designed for formal dances, dinner parties, and political engagements. There wasn't anything here that was even remotely suitable to send to someone whose home had been destroyed. Then her eyes settled on Sophia's comm bracelet.

Cora picked up the small bracelet and sat on the floor. Several months ago, she'd figured out how to crack into Sophia's bracelet and view her personal messages. At the time, she'd wanted to understand why her sister had chosen to end her life.

Activating the bracelet, she created a tiny floating screen and began scanning through love messages between Sophia and someone with the initial 'D.' A sick feeling formed in the pit of her stomach as she skimmed through the messages. Her chest tightened as she thought of her sister cheating on Harold, who'd been a kind and loving husband.

"Cora? Are you here?" Brian called.

She frowned, disappointed she didn't have more time to examine Sophia's comm bracelet.

"Your Aunt said you were up here. Do you want help?" Brian called again.

Cora heard his footsteps pacing closer, and she shoved Sophia's bracelet behind her back. A moment later, the door slid open.

"There you are. Why didn't you answer?"

Brian sauntered into the room with a grin and plopped onto the floor, facing her.

"Aunt asked me to collect clothes for the workers on Mars," Cora said, shoving the bracelet further behind her.

"I know..." He rolled his eyes. "I tried to explain it'd be better to send credits, but..."

"She wouldn't listen." Her mouth twitched as she detected his broadcast merriment, but she wanted to be alone to think. "Is there something you wanted?"

"Yes, to invite you to lunch." His smile faded. "But you're up to something."

"W-What? No," Her eyes avoided his and glided over the mountain of clothes. "I am trying to figure out which dress is appropriate. How many formal dances do the miners attend, any-way?"

He followed her gaze and then locked eyes with her. "You're up to something."

She chuckled, "I'm the Feeler around here, so how do you know when I'm hiding something?"

"Simple." His face split into a lopsided grin. "I've known you for ten years. You were never good at hiding your feelings."

"Fine." Her face wrinkled with a worried expression. "I promised Harold I would look into what happened to Sophia. I still think she took her own life because of this." She pulled Sophia's bracelet from behind her back and handed it to him. "Look at this, but please don't tell Harold."

"Sure." He glanced at her with one eyebrow raised as if asking a question, then studied the messages displayed on a tiny floating screen. While he read, Cora stood and sorted through Sophia's gowns. She held up a short orange dress—she'd never seen Sophia in this dress. There was so much she didn't know about her sister.

Brian sighed and leaned forward. "I can hardly believe what I'm reading. How long did this go on behind Uncle's back?"

Cora sensed his disappointment flowing in waves.

"I'm sorry, Brian." She tossed the orange dress back on the pile and sat on the floor again. "Maybe I shouldn't have told you."

"It's okay. I'd rather know than not know," he said. "Did Uncle suspect anything?"

"He had no idea while she was alive," she said. "None of us knew at the time. I'm not even sure how she pulled it off. This went on for six months, and they met several times a week."

"Why were you reading this now?" he asked as he handed Sophia's bracelet to her. "She passed away almost a year ago."

"Well... I'm not sure where to begin," she said. "A year ago, right after Sophia... Anyway, I stumbled across her comm inside a sealed package from the EGS, buried under a mound of clothes. Harold asked me to move her clothes to this storage room. He couldn't stand..."

"I remember—he was so upset," he said while his voice caught on the last few words. "Poor Uncle."

"I thought Sophia had ended her life, and I wanted to understand why." Cora put the bracelet on the floor in front of her and stood to continue sorting through Sophia's dresses.

Brian remained sitting, but he started collecting and sorting through her shoes. "It took me a few hours to break into her comm, and that's when I found the messages." She picked up a shimmering gold dress. "Sophia wore a lot of gold, didn't she?"

"She looked good in gold," he said, and held up a pair of matching shoes. "I think I saw her wear these shoes with that dress."

Cora hung the gold dress neatly on a rack and placed the matching gold shoes underneath. "Anyway, the messages fit with the EGS's suicide theory. Especially the last message."

"Yes, I see what you mean," he said as he knit his eyebrows. "'I need you... I can't go on... I won't live without you.'"

"Exactly!" she said as she turned to select a green dress with no back and a slit on the right side. "I tried to bring these messages up with Harold a few times. He knew about them, but he got so upset."

"I feel so sorry for him."

"Me too. I never brought it up again," Cora said, and sighed.

Brian lifted shimmery green slippers that may have matched the green dress in Cora's hands. She glanced at them a moment, then shook her head. Brian returned them to the sorting pile. "What changed now?"

Cora hesitated. *How much can I tell Brian?* she thought.

Brian turned to Cora and met her eyes. "I promise I won't tell."

"A couple of days ago when we talked about Etta, I told you she used her Seer abilities and witnessed Sophia's murderer." She raked her fingers through her curly hair. "What I didn't tell you is now Harold's determined to find Sophia's killer, and I've promised to help."

"Uncle told me his idea that someone murdered Sophia a few months ago. I think he's right. She didn't have the personality to do it. Uncle thinks she was too full of life to end her life." He frowned. "But I think she was a selfish, narcissistic twit. It would've never occurred to her to end it all. Those messages are all melodrama." He huffed. "I couldn't stand her, but Uncle loved her."

"Yeah, he seems so lost without her," she said.

"What I don't like is you two looking for the killer." He set his mouth in a grim line. "I'm going to talk to him."

"What're you going to tell him? 'The wife you loved cheated on you and that may have gotten her killed?'"

"No, not that." He ran a hand through his jet-black hair. "He needs to report Etta to the EGS because she must know the killer."

"So, you mean the same EGS that has already closed Sophia's case with a ruling of suicide?" She shook her head. "Unless you have direct proof against Etta, they aren't going to reopen the case."

She turned to a pile of dresses and handed the short orange one to him.

Brian stared at the dress for a moment, thinking.

"I still think this is risky. I'm calling the EGS myself."

"Okay, that's fair," Cora said as she sorted through a pile of handbags. Many of them matched the shoes. "I went with Harold to meet the McCarthys and Tristan Quimby. Harold thinks that someone at the table killed Sophia. Probably with some military tech."

"How would anyone at that table get their hands on military tech?" He frowned.

"The McCarthys have government ties with indirect links to the military." Cora started arranging the bags and purses by color. "It's a long shot, but there's a chance."

"I see," he said, hanging a little orange dress and absently pulled a long black dress from a pile. He shook it out and placed it on the rack. "So, what happened with the McCarthys and Quimby?"

"Wesley acted a little... uneasy, but *Vivian* broadcast fury. I nearly lost myself." She sighed. "She's dangerous—she showed none of that emotion. In fact, she appeared light-hearted."

"You lowered your shield?" His eyebrows furrowed. "I thought that wasn't safe?"

"It should've been safe—there were only four of us in the room." She shivered, recalling the waves of rage and the room twisting until she resumed shielding. "I need to be more careful around her."

"I wonder what that was about?" he said, hanging an emerald green dress next to the black one.

"Not sure, but the point is how well she hid it." She sorted through a new pile of dresses. "When I've encountered people like that in the past, they were disturbed. Not normal. Sick even."

"I see..." He turned to face her. "Are you saying she might be a suspect?"

"Maybe... It's hard to say right now." She pulled a navy dress out of the pile and handed it to him.

"They're both in the public light so much, they must be used to hiding their genuine feelings." He bent and selected a pair of black shoes from the shoe pile and placed them under the long black dress.

"I didn't realize you're so good at accessorizing," Cora said with a grin, trying to lighten the dark mood.

"I'm a man of many talents," Brian said in a level voice. A second later, they both chuckled. She hung another short black dress, and he hung a gold pants suit next to it.

"Tristan Quimby seemed the most suspicious," Cora said. "He actually tried to bribe Harold."

"Bribe?" Brian asked, as he turned and focused his gray-blue eyes on Cora.

"Essentially, he'd only come to the party if Harold purchased the paintings Sophia promised to buy a year ago." She shivered. "I shielded myself around him, but I'm glad I couldn't feel his actual emotions."

"Hmm... I think I've only met him once or twice."

"Yesterday, I met him for the second time. There's something slimy about him."

He scratched his head. "So, why were you looking through Sophia's messages now?"

"Well, when I read them before, they seemed to point towards suicide. I thought she'd taken something before the dinner and then died at the table. I thought 'D' was someone at the table. Also, that would be Sophia's melodramatic style."

"I don't buy it," Brian said. "She could've taken something to get sick and cause a scene, but not kill herself."

She paused, scanning Sophia's bags.

"That's a good point," Cora said. "Now, I wonder if the messages point the finger at a murderer. Although, I don't see how anyone could have tampered with her drink or food."

Cora carefully stacked matching bags into piles while he chose another black dress and hung it on the rack.

"So, you must think that 'D' could be Wesley McCarthy or Tristan Quimby," Brian said. "The only trouble is neither of them has a name that starts with 'D'."

"No, that'd be too simple," she said. "Sophia and deception went well together."

She moved the small stack of bags to a nearby shelf.

Brian gazed at her with a frown. "I know Sophia was horrible to you, and somehow always got away with it."

Cora glanced at Brian before returning to another stack of bags. Her face grew a little warm. "I should've been able to defend myself earlier from her."

"You were also a kid with no protection from your parents," Brian said in a gentle voice. "By the time I met you, you could defend yourself."

"Sophia taught me a lot. Not that she intended to," she said with a mirthless laugh. "I'm just happy I didn't turn out like her." She took a deep breath. "In any case, we need a list of possible suspects."

"Well... If we start with family, that'd be Uncle, Aunt Ferna, you, and Oliver," he said. "If we include friends, we could start with Tristan, but the list could build to hundreds of people."

"Last year, Oliver was in Lunar City and Aunt Ferna had another dinner engagement. So, we're down to Harold and me."

"Okay, if we're to follow Uncle's lead, the murderer was at the table, so the main suspects are Wesley, Vivian, and Tristan," he said. "It's not likely to be a family member."

"Everyone at the table is technically a suspect. That includes you, me, Sophia, Harold, and Ruby." Cora pulled her thick dark curls behind her ear. "I included Sophia because she could've ended her life."

"Okay, what's my motive?" Brian asked with a half-smile.

"I don't know..." Cora said while scratching her head. "Why were you at Sophia's party?"

"Uncle Harold." Brian stifled a chuckle. "Don't take this the wrong way, but I truly disliked your sister. I hated the way she treated Uncle. Also, others at the table didn't care for her."

"Who else?" she asked.

"I wouldn't be at all surprised if Wesley only tolerated her." He spoke in a soft voice. "She'd this smarmy way of taking over conversations."

"I found it hard to spend time around her, too." She turned to a new pile of dress pants—the flowy comfortable pants Sophia wore around the house. Even her comfortable wear would be too flimsy to help the miners.

"Maybe her redeeming quality was her intelligence."

"No, not intelligent exactly... I tried to speak to her many times. She never seemed to have an original thought. She never had an opinion based on information she'd taken the time to gather." He paused for a moment, peering at the ceiling. "I'd call her cunning... or manipulative... or shrewd. Basically, not nice." Brian grabbed Cora's hand. "Come, let's go to lunch."

"But, Aunt..." She let Brian lead her out of the storage room.

"I know she'll be upset, but I think we'll both feel better after some food." He stepped out of the room.

"Can't help thinking about Harold," she said, following him down the hall.

"Me too. But I agree with Uncle." Brian ambled toward the antigrav lift. "Someone killed her."

"I think..." Cora pulled her hand from Brian's while they walked together toward the antigrav lift. "She took her own life, but I'm open to other ideas."

"On a different note, have you thought over what I said?" He glanced at her.

"You mean about my game? I think you're right." Cora took steady steps down the third-floor hall toward the antigrav lift.

"Wait—" Brian stopped in his tracks, a grin on his face. "What was that? Could you please repeat—I want to record your words."

She rolled her eyes.

"I want to start in gradual steps," she said. "I feel like I'm handing over my firstborn."

Brian covered his mouth, hiding a chuckle. "Okay, what'd you like to do first?"

She glared at him, but her mouth twitched. "You know I can still kick you out of my game."

He saluted like a soldier. "Yes, ma'am."

She chortled, and they both continued towards the lift.

"Let's start by bringing your friends onto the server to get some feedback. But I want to know who they are and what they do for a living. I don't want to accidentally invite a competitor."

"Good. When do you want to start?" He reached the antigrav lift and waved his hand over the sensor, causing the door to slide open. They both stepped in.

"Let's start after the commemorative dinner, in about a week."

"Sounds good." A moment later, he stepped out of the lift on the first floor. "The Tasty Noodle? I haven't eaten there in a couple of weeks."

"Sounds good. But we ate there a few days ago." She giggled.

CHAPTER 8

The next day, Cora stood at the fountain behind her home—her favorite feature in the back garden. She gazed into the rippling water shadowed by a statue of the goddess, Askae. An ancient religion had depicted her as an old wrinkled woman with gnarled fingers who bestowed gifts to her followers. The gifts both helped and harmed the recipients, teaching them about the dual nature of their abilities. Askovians had been named after Askae and thought of their powers as gifts from the goddess. However, Cora rarely came across an Askovian that remembered the dual nature of their abilities.

A chime from her comm bracelet broke through her thoughts. She swiped a hand over the bracelet, starting a vidchat.

"Good morning, Brian," she said as his image appeared on the floating screen.

"Hey, Cora. How's the garden today?" Brian asked.

"Beautiful as usual." Cora's eyes scanned the fountain, walkway leading into thicker brush, manicured flower beds, and birds flitting from tree to tree. "Can you hear that warbler?" She grinned. "Wish I could stay out here forever."

"I could join you if you like." He leaned away from the screen.

"I'd like your company, but not here." Her smile slid from her face and she sighed. "Would you join me at the Briny Club in about an hour?"

"Still trying to find Sophia's murderer?" He leaned an elbow on the table in front of him.

"Yes. I really don't believe any of us could have killed Sophia. That leaves Wesley, Vivian, and Tristan. My plan is to interview each of them," she said, turning toward the house.

"Do you want help with them?" he asked.

"I might. I'll let you know," she said, ambling away from the fountain. "I also want to talk to Etta, but her information is so well hidden, I'd have to talk to the Spencer family. Harold won't like that, and so I've settled for talking to some people defrauded by Etta."

"What do you want me to do?" His eyebrows knit as his blue-gray eyes bored into hers.

"I made an appointment two hours from now at the Briny Club." She stopped pacing. "Would you come with me? I was hoping you might notice something I miss when I talk to them."

"Yes, I see," he nodded. "I still think this is dangerous, but at least you're not talking directly to Etta."

"I'm trying to be as thorough as possible so I can convince Harold to just let this investigation go." *That way we can all go back to how things were for the past year*, she thought.

"I really don't think you can change his mind, but I'm willing to help," he said. "Hmm... I've been meaning to try the special there this week. I'll pick you up in an hour and a half."

"Oh, you don't have..." Cora spoke to an empty space. He'd ended the vidchat.

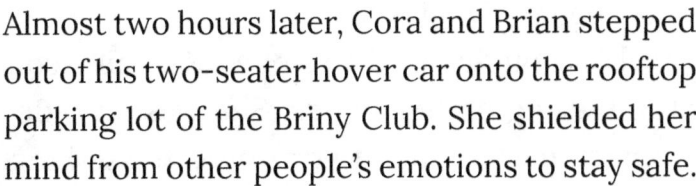

Almost two hours later, Cora and Brian stepped out of his two-seater hover car onto the rooftop parking lot of the Briny Club. She shielded her mind from other people's emotions to stay safe.

They'd both changed into more formal clothes suitable for the Club. Cora wore a pale gray dress that flowed around her legs while Brian wore a tan jumpsuit. The roof was full of other floating cars, but they were alone as they took the antigrav lift down to the third floor.

"We need to go this way," she said quietly, stepping out of the antigrav lift and turning left. She paced over a deep red carpet lining a long hall with gold trim around the doors to each flat. As she ambled, she glanced at the fine art spaced along the hall until she reached Ms. Vallencott's door. She waved her hand over the door sensor and waited. A moment later, someone answered.

"Hello. May I help you?" the sensor voice said.

"Hello. Ms. Vallencott? I'm Cora Brimble. We spoke in a vidchat yesterday."

"Oh, yes. Come in. Come in." The door slid open, and a puff of warm, perfume-scented air washed over them.

Cora and Brian sauntered into the apartment, entering her living room.

"Oh, I thought you'd be alone." Ms. Vallencott stood wringing her hands. She was an older woman, maybe around Etta's age, dressed in a floral dress suitable for a tea party. Her white hair was up in a loose bun, but her dark brown eyes studied Brian.

"Ms. Vallencott. I'm sorry I should have explained. This is Brian Farris. He's a friend helping me to find out more about Etta. I hope it's okay for him to stay."

"If you don't feel comfortable, I can wait in the restaurant downstairs," Brian said with a soft smile.

"Well... Harold asked me to talk to you as a favor." Ms. Vallencott turned from Cora to Brian and studied him for a moment. "I suppose it's okay. Have a seat." She gestured to two overstuffed sofas facing each other. She'd filled the entire room with knickknacks, furniture, paintings, and books. Cora surveyed the books before she took her seat.

"I see you've noticed my collection," Ms. Vallencott grinned. "I've been collecting since I was twelve years old. And..." She paused as she took her seat. "I've read every one."

"Congratulations," Cora grinned, truly impressed. There must have been several hundred books along the walls and stacked on the floor.

"Would you like something to drink?" Ms. Vallencott waved her hand over a sensor on her coffee table. "I was just about to make tea."

"Tea would be fine." Cora nodded and glanced at Brian, who nodded as well.

Cora and Ms. Vallencott sipped their tea while Brian munched on a bright pink cookie.

"I was quite surprised when Harold contacted me. He said you're looking into something for him," Ms. Vallencott said.

Brian reached for a second cookie when Cora put down her cup.

"Yes, it's related to Etta Johanson. I'll try not to take up too much of your time," Cora said. "Ms. Vallencott, would you tell me about your session with her?"

"My grandson introduced me to her. He's friends with Tristan, who's friends with Etta." She shifted uncomfortably in the chair. "I met Etta at lunch downstairs several weeks ago. I thought it was a chance meeting, but my grandson later confessed that he arranged it." She paused and surveyed her teacup for a moment. "Etta said her abilities could help me reach my husband Archie from the other side. Now that I say this all out loud, it sounds so stupid."

"You must've missed your husband." Cora lowered her shield in tiny steps, hoping to sense something more from the conversation. So far, she only perceived small sprays of embarrassment.

"We were married for thirty years." Ms. Vallencott gave her head a small shake. "Etta came to this room and held a seance. I'd never been to one before, and it seemed so exciting. Archie came through, his real voice ringing through the room. I was amazed at first, but then I began talking to him, and some things he said didn't make sense."

"Can you give me some examples?" Cora asked.

"Archie talked of the many dinners we'd had downstairs. But I moved to Tymal after Archie passed away. My family is from here, but Archie'd never set foot in this building." She wrung her hands again. "Oh, I feel like such a fool."

"Please don't feel bad." Brian sat upright in his seat. "Etta's a professional con artist who has fooled dozens of people."

"Did you tell Etta about the inconsistencies with Archie?"

Ms. Vallencott's face hardened. "I certainly did. As time wore on, Archie's voice sounded the same, but the inconsistencies increased. I eventually confronted her, and she became quite angry. We ended up yelling at each other... It didn't end well."

"Who did you tell about the seance with Etta?" Brian asked.

"I started with the management of this club, and I got her permanently barred. I told anyone who would listen, my grandson, and Tristan, although I think he was in on it."

"Did the Spencers contact you?" Cora asked.

"Ah... Um. No." Ms. Vallencott took a sip of tea and didn't meet Cora's eyes.

Cora sensed the lie right away.

"I'm not trying to harm you or any of the Spencer family. As I said, I'm looking into a personal matter for Harold, and I want to understand Etta better." She paused for a moment, surveying Ms. Vallencott's broadcast emotions as they tumbled between confusion and unease. "Would you tell me what's bothering you?"

"Um... They gave me a lot of credits to ignore what happened with Etta. They made it clear not to tell anyone, but that was after I'd told all my friends here." Ms. Vallencott wrung her hands again.

"I understand. I won't reveal anything of our conversation to the Spencers. Really, I just want to understand what happened," Cora said.

After a momentary pause, Ms. Vallencott frowned. "I was furious with Etta, but really what's hurt is my pride. I can't believe I fell for such a scam." She sighed. "Like I said, I reported her to the management, told my friends, and then the Spencer family contacted me. I haven't heard from them or Etta since."

"One more thing, do you happen to know who or even how Etta created Archie's voice?" Brian asked.

"Not sure, but I think my grandson gave them old vidchats with my Archie." She sighed. "Tristan used the recordings to change his voice to Archie's."

Cora sensed Ms. Vallencott's jitters when she mentioned her grandson. She hoped for Ms. Vallencott's sake, her grandson wasn't more involved than providing copies of Archie's vidchats. "Thank you so much for your time. If you think of something we didn't talk about, would you send me a message?"

"Of course. Um. May I ask what all this is about?" Ms. Vallencott nibbled absently at the edge of a cookie.

"It's a personal concern that Harold asked me to look into. I wish I could say more, but I don't have his permission." Cora glanced at Brian. "Do you have any more questions?"

He shook his head and stood. "Thank you for your time."

———————— 🚀 ————————

Fifteen minutes later, Cora and Brian sat at a dining table on the ground floor of the Briny Club. Before them were two plates of coconut shrimp, lemon and garlic rice, and broccoli. A small smile crept on her face as she inhaled the pungent aromas.

"I know what you mean." Brian grinned. "I haven't had this in... maybe a year."

"It's been longer for me." Cora picked up her fork and stabbed a shrimp. "The food at the Briny is amazing. I wonder what they do differently."

"Mmm..." Brian stuffed a shrimp into his mouth.

She put a fork full of rice in her mouth and chewed as the tangy flavors coated her tongue. The sound of the other diners talking floated across their table while she glanced out of the wall of windows at the sidewalk. A mom with a small child drifted by on their way to the nearby stores. A group of three teens sauntered onto the walkway, each with an ice cream cone.

"Pardon. Are you Cora Brimble?"

Cora turned to find a tall, thin man with wrinkled brown skin and a cloud of white hair standing at the table.

Cora wiped her mouth with her napkin and put her fork down on her empty plate. "Yes. Are you Mr. Washington?"

"Please call me Omar." He gestured at the seat. "May I?"

"Of course. Please have a seat." She turned to Brian. "This is Brian Farris. He's helping me to understand more about Etta."

"That name's familiar. Is your dad Benjamin Farris?" he said in a deep, rumbly voice.

"Yes," Brian said, a little surprised.

"I taught him at school," Omar chuckled.

"Really? I'll tell my dad I ran into you," Brian said with a small smile.

The smile faded from Omar's face as he turned to the matter at hand.

"Harold asked me to talk to you about Etta and her visions. I agreed to meet with you because I wanted you to understand Etta better," he coughed and summoned a nearby robot.

"May I help you?" The robotic waiter spoke in a soft, detached voice.

"A glass of water, please." Omar coughed again.

"Right away." The robot waiter turned and floated toward the kitchen.

"Just a moment, Ms. Brimble—" Omar said.

"Please, call me Cora," she said, interrupting Omar

The robot returned with a glass of water.

"Just what I needed." He took a sip and exhaled. "You see, basically, Etta's a good kid. She just sometimes loses her way."

Cora stifled a giggle—she would've never thought of Etta as a kid. "What do you mean?"

"A couple of years ago, we dated. I thought things were going well, but Etta was always playing her games. She makes a prediction and when it doesn't come true, her clients get mad." Omar shrugged a shoulder. "Make sense."

"Why aren't you dating now?" Brian asked.

"I'm getting there. Don't rush me." Omar said with an edge to his voice. He took a sip and exhaled, surveying the tabletop.

Cora and Brian exchanged a glance as a new robot arrived to take their plates away.

"So, when we dated, Etta had a vision that Agnes, one of her clients, would come into a large pile of credits. This actually happened after Agnes's uncle passed away. It surprised everyone, *including* Etta. Then word got out about Etta's vision." Omar took another sip. "Other family members heard of Etta's prediction and began to suspect Agnes killed her uncle. Then Global Security got involved and Agnes was driven into debt, hiring attorneys to defend herself. Agnes won her case, but it meant little at that point. Even after her inheritance, Agnes was still trying to pay off the remaining debt."

"Wow! I heard about Agnes when the story first appeared in the Global News." Brian leaned back in his chair. "I didn't follow up to see what happened to her."

"I don't quite see how you fit in, though," Cora turned to Omar.

Omar grimaced. "Yes, well... Agnes sued Etta for the remaining debt. Etta asked Mabel Spencer and her two sisters for help. They refused." He took a sip of water. "Etta stole credits from me and gave them to Agnes. I found out about it and Etta and I argued. Ended up breaking up. All of that happened right here in this room." He paused and surveyed the other diners.

"I never heard about that." Cora's eyebrows furrowed. "I've looked through many of the minutes of this club and found nothing about that."

"The minutes of the club are available to all club members, but the Spencers couldn't have their good name tarnished." Omar chuckled. "They got the official minutes changed, paid off Agnes, and moved Etta out of the Briny Club."

"I'm amazed. I've never heard of this," Brian said with raised eyebrows.

"Why didn't the Spencers erase the complaints from you and Ms. Vallencott?" Cora asked.

Omar chortled. "They couldn't. The EGS controls that system. If you want something removed, you have to prove that it's wrong, invalid, or has corrupted data." His laughter died down. "I still care about Etta and don't want to see her harmed. She's a good person who sometimes makes stupid decisions."

"Thanks for helping us." Brian shook Omar's hand.

"I wanted you to understand Etta's character a little better," Omar said.

Cora shook Omar's hand. "You've been very helpful."

CHAPTER 9

Cora woke early the next morning, slipped out of her pajamas, and put on a comfortable top and pants set. She ate breakfast in her room while studying the messages from 'D' on Sophia's comm. She had cracked the encryption months ago, and was now able to read the messages. But she wondered which of Sophia's friends would know how to hide them. Most of Sophia's friends were artists, poets, and writers, who had limited technical abilities.

She tried to access the source of the messages, and found the sender, location, and path through the Net all encrypted. She sighed at the thought of having to decrypt the source information. She then studied the date and time, which 'D' didn't hide.

Cora selected a few buttons on her own bracelet and a new floating screen appeared over her desk. Tapping on the display screen caused it to be filled with decryption symbols, which she arranged in several specific sequences. She launched the routine and waited. Glaring at the hovering screen, she watched the symbols slowly rotate and rearrange themselves on her screen, hoping they'd show the message's owner or location soon. She hoped it would at least show a physical address. The decryption routine could take several minutes or a few days, depending on the complexity of the encryption. After five minutes of nothing happening, she gave up and accepted that she'd have to wait for the decryption routine to complete.

She pressed a button on her bracelet and created a second screen next to the first. Tapping on the screen, she revealed her Mystery Adventure game. She worked on a new puzzle that required players to use the underside of the stairs. Cora grinned as she tried to imagine Brian trying to figure out how to counteract gravity.

A moment later, her bracelet chimed, and she stared at the name hovering over the bracelet. She activated the vidchat as her mouth twitched, trying to fight a smile. "Hello, I was just thinking about you."

"That means you've come up with another diabolical puzzle that'll take me ages to figure out," Brian said, munching on clear green cubes.

"I have no idea how you can eat that candy." Cora wrinkled her nose. "They taste like toilet chemicals."

"Are you kidding? They're the best." Brian raised one eyebrow. "And how do you know what toilet chemicals taste like?"

"You know what I mean. They smell the same as toilet chemicals and—" A new chime sounded, interrupting her. She turned to stare at the decryption screen she'd created to trace Sophia's first message's origin. "Wow! All the way there?"

"What're you doing?" He swallowed the last of the green cubes. "Coding?"

"Something else—" She paused with mock horror on her face. "No, not another one."

He snickered as he opened a fresh bag of orange cubes and sniffed.

"The orange ones are worse than the green," she giggled. "I think you need your nose checked out."

"Mmm. Delicious!" He chuckled. "I'll save some for you."

"Eww." She made an exaggerated shiver.

"Okay, if you weren't coding, why the chime?" He popped an orange cube into his mouth.

"Oh, that..." She turned and glanced at the monitor. "I'm just curious about something. I still think Sophia ended her life, but I just want to make sure I've checked all possibilities."

"So, which clue are you following now?" He asked and ate another orange cube.

"I created a program to decrypt the trail one of Sophia's comm messages took through the Net. The program chimes when it finds a new leg of the trail." Her program chimed again, and she turned to examine her program's progress. "It's strange... When I decrypted the sender, it only showed 'D'. But, the location is somewhat easy to figure out. It's as if two different programmers worked on this message."

"Hmmm. It could be the same person worked on that message, but..." Brian paused and focused on his ceiling. "Maybe... not too competent."

"I don't know. Standard encryption would've been better than this." She glanced at the decryption screen.

"That's what I mean by 'not too competent.'" He chuckled. "When you figure out the message's source, what're you going to do?"

"I thought I might take a little trip," she said with a sly smile. "You wanna go?"

"When do we leave?" he asked, as he closed the bag of orange cubes.

"Why don't you make your way over here?" She peeked over her shoulder. "I think I've got a few more minutes before the decryption's done."

"See you in a bit," he chortled, and a moment later, his image disappeared.

Cora grinned and turned to face the decryption screen.

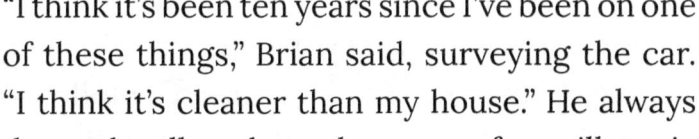

"I think it's been ten years since I've been on one of these things," Brian said, surveying the car. "I think it's cleaner than my house." He always dressed well, and now he wore a faux silk tunic and voluminous matching pants.

Cora and Brian stood in a public passenger train heading toward Rosedel, an independent district of Tymal. Passengers filled the train's ten connecting cars to capacity, about five hundred people, in the mornings, but Cora prepared by shielding herself from the passengers' emotions.

Cora chuckled. "We're going to the *Rosedel* District. They have their own security and cleaning crew—everything will be spotless." She wore a pale green tailored faux silk top and pants suit that allowed her to blend in with business class. Nobody wore clothing from animals any longer—factories manufactured fabric from chemicals and plants.

"They've their own everything," he said. "I don't know why they need to operate like their own independent country."

Everyone called Cora and Brian's transportation a train, but it didn't run on rails any longer. Instead, it used a series of antigrav blocks attached to the passenger cars, causing them to hover over the rocky ground. In addition, it used its own internal navigation to follow a set path throughout the city. A sophisticated AI named LARA maintained the schedule while avoiding pedestrians, animals, and other traffic.

"Yeah, Sophia called them the elite's elite." A smile and then a frown flitted across her face.

"Are you okay?" He asked in a soft voice.

"Oh... I still hate her, but sometimes I miss her." She sighed. "Doesn't make sense."

"Emotions don't always make sense. They just are."

Cora glanced at Brian before gazing out of the window. She pulled her jacket tighter around her shoulders, feeling vulnerable. A moment later, the train slowed, bringing her out of her reverie. She glanced at her bracelet and followed the electronic trail out of the train.

The Rosedel District looked like an artist's rendering of utopia. It was a planned community designed from the ground up for walking and public transportation. She stepped on a mowed, grassy walkway lined on both sides by shops, hotels, and a few government buildings and wide enough for four hover cars to float side-by-side. The architecture of the nearby buildings consisted of modern, clean lines. Their slanted roofs allowed rain to fall into beautiful oval pools that blended into the landscaping. The asymmetrical windows reminded her of a kids' game designed to teach children shapes and their names.

"Mmm... Well, at least it smells good." She inhaled a faint floral aroma. "We can walk to our destination." She examined the electronic trail.

"This way." Still expecting traffic, she glanced up and down the street, and set off to her left.

"Wow. It's been years since I visited." He studied the buildings and people ambling and drifting on the street with them.

"I know. I think I was in my early twenties, but I can't remember what I did here." She rechecked her bracelet.

They walked in silence for a few more minutes when Cora repositioned the bracelet's map and turned right. With Brian behind her, she followed a narrow path between two large hotels. She spied dignitaries from other Earth nations, Lunar City, and Anteros.

As they continued to walk, with the two hotels behind them, the buildings fell away to reveal a huge, gleaming lake.

"Funny. I can't remember the lake from my last visit," she said.

"It's a natural lake, but it's helped by several filtration systems," he said. "That's what makes it look so pristine."

"Okay, we need to turn right again." She started off. "There are several small apartments buried in between those massive hotels."

"I remember. Many celebrities and politicians have private homes and apartments here," Brian said. "The corporations who own the large hotels tried to get them removed, but it didn't work."

"Umm hmm. We're nearly there," Cora said, staring at her bracelet's map. Several minutes later, she stopped walking and surveyed a bland apartment complex with only four units. The building looked well-maintained, but it needed updating.

"The message came from that unit." She pointed to an upstairs unit on the right.

"It's a bit disappointing compared to its view." He glanced from the building's facade to the lake. "So, how are we going to get in?"

"Before we left for Rosedel, I found the rental agency for this complex," she said while maneuvering her bracelet's map. "It turns out they're not too far from here."

"What do you think you're going to do?" he asked with a chuckle. "Walk in and ask for a list of people who've rented that unit?"

Cora turned and walked back the way they'd come. "Sort of." She smirked. "I'll just gently help them share their information."

"You mean steal it." He shook his head.

"I've helped corporations 'share' their information loads of times." She snickered. "I never used the information for nefarious reasons. In this case, we're looking for a potential murderer."

Cora and Brian returned to the main walking path where the train dropped them off. This time, they continued past four more large hotels until they reached a quaint set of small business buildings. Following her map, she stopped at a door with a sign that read 'Lakeside Rentals.'

"This is the real estate office 'D' used." Cora glanced to the right and left. She spied a Lunar clothing specialty store on the right and a currency exchange for Lunar and Martian credits.

"Aren't we going in?" Brian asked.

"Not yet." Cora turned to examine the buildings across the street. "Let's go to the cafe." She stepped onto the large busy grassy walkway and dodged children, business people, and a few Lunar and Martian dignitaries. Brian kept pace with her with little effort as they made their way to the 'Caffeine Cabin.'

Cora and Brian stepped into the large cafe, and she inhaled a wild mixture of coffee, fruit, and sugar. Even the decor comprised a kaleidoscope of colors and textures from the deepest jungles on Earth to the barren landscapes of the moon, culminating in the multiple shades of red-orange found on Mars. Even though many people filled the cafe, dampers that cancel sound vibrations between tables allowed her to converse easily with Brian.

"Do you want coffee?" he asked as he headed to the line.

"Yes." Cora scanned the seating areas. Heading toward a table facing the street and Lakeside Rentals, she changed her bracelet's display to private and opened a coding screen. She created new symbols and rearranged them on her coding screen, creating her sniffer program. Its goal comprised making a deep dive into databases to extract information. She started her program.

"Well, at least the service is fairly quick," he said, joining her at the table with two cups. Her cup contained black coffee, and she grinned as she took a sip.

"Mmm. Good," she said and then gazed at his concoction. "What in the world is that?"

"Martian Sunrise," he said with a grin. "It's filled with pineapple, orange juice, grenadine, and lemon juice to cut the sweetness."

"You're kidding?" She folded her arms. "Brian, all of those flavors are from Earth. What makes that drink Martian?"

"Oh, I forgot to mention the pinch of Martian salt mined from the ancient seas." He took a sip. "Mmm. It's so good. The salt helps balance the flavors."

"It's just a gimmick to sell more drinks." She took another sip of coffee.

"I know, but it's fun to pretend I'm actually there with every sip." He chuckled.

Cora rolled her eyes.

"Speaking of scams," he said, "do you need more time to get ready?"

"I'm not scamming anybody," she said in a low voice, glancing around the cafe. "And keep your voice down. I'm running a test here in the cafe to see what I come up with."

Turning to her private screen, she began looking through the data. While they talked, her sniffer program absorbed the identifying data of the customers using the Caffeine Cabin's internal network. Satisfied that everything worked well, she paused her program and deleted the data she'd gathered.

"Okay, I'm done. Whenever you're ready," she said.

"What're you going to say to get them to hand over the data?" he asked as he took his last sip of Martian Sunrise.

"Don't worry, I've got that all planned out." She stood, heading to the door with a small smile playing on her face.

They crossed the road and entered Lakeside Rentals. Cora activated her sniffer program as she took in the large room, decorated like a lakeside cabana. Three desks, each manned by an agent, stood in the center of an office space adorned with faux banana leaves. She paused, a little disoriented to find humans working in this business. Many businesses in Rosedel prided themselves on personalized customer service. This allowed them to charge hefty premiums for their service. She strolled toward an agent who'd just completed a vidchat. As she reached his desk, he greeted her with a smile, revealing the most perfect teeth she'd ever seen. His teeth lined his mouth in a perfectly straight line and almost gleamed with a piercing light.

"Good afternoon, madam. Sir. Please have a seat." Perfect teeth gestured to the two seats on the opposite side of his desk. Cora and Brian took them.

"I'm Greg. How may I help you?" he asked.

"I'm looking for an apartment," Cora said as she tried to stop herself from staring at his teeth. "Something with one or two bedrooms facing the Lake."

"Lakeside rentals are very hard to find," Greg said, swiping his hand over his desk resulting in a list of rentals appearing on a screen floating over his desk. "I assume the apartment is for the two of you?"

"No!" Cora said, stronger than she'd intended, and then turned pink. "Just for me."

Brian raised an eyebrow but said nothing.

"Actually, I have a particular unit in mind." Cora shifted uncomfortably in her chair.

"Send the address," Greg said with his gleaming white teeth.

Cora waved a hand over her bracelet and a new screen appeared over Greg's desk.

"Just a moment while I access an updated list," Greg said. He closed his original screen and opened a new one with a larger list of rentals. Greg moved the address Cora had sent to his new list, and a chime sounded as the addresses turned red. "It seems this is one of our units, but it's rented."

"That's fine." Cora needed him to access their database of rentals so her sniffer could capture his information. "Can you find other rentals similar to the one I showed you?"

"Well... Let me see something." Greg cleared the current screen. "I'll use search parameters created from the address you provided." A second later, a new chime sounded. "Seven new apartments are a close match to the apartment you provided."

"Wonderful!" A grin crept across her face. While she was here for the address of Sophia's admirer, she had been toying with the idea of moving out of the family home. Originally, she'd wanted to distance herself from Sophia. After her sister passed, she had begun to love her family home, but she still liked the idea of living in a place all her own. "Which apartments are close to the lake?"

"Ah... None of them." A momentary frown marred his face. "It turns out that rental unit was the only new one in the past twelve months. Most families keep their apartments and pass them to their children."

"I'm surprised. Why would someone hold on to a rental for so long instead of purchasing?"

"The location is iconic. Violet Lake has been a draw for celebrities, politicians, and wealthy business owners for at least a hundred years. The closest apartment is a short train ride away."

"Well, okay. I had my heart set on the Rosedel District." She stood and glanced toward Brian. "I think it's time we head back."

"I'm very sorry I couldn't help you," Greg said.

"Thank you for your time," she replied, stepped toward the door, and out onto the large grassy walkway.

"Where to next?" Brian asked as he strolled beside her.

"Home to check on my sniffer," Cora said with a broad grin. "I left a copy of my program just in case I need more information from them." Brian rolled his eyes, and Cora giggled. "I won't steal their data or damage anything. I'm just trying to prove that Sophia ended her life when 'D' broke things off."

CHAPTER 10

C ora and Brian headed for the train home. They reached the platform for the train just as it floated to a stop. She glanced at the sky—the sun hung low on the horizon, and she shivered as the temperature dropped. Bryan swiped his bracelet by the door as he stepped onto the train, and a moment later Cora swiped hers. A loud, discordant sound alerted everyone that the train didn't accept her credits. Several people turned to stare, but Cora studied her bracelet, wondering why she'd received the loud alert.

"What's the matter?" Brian turned to step off the train.

"I don't know..." Cora pressed the same button on her bracelet again. "The train won't take my credits, but I don't see an error message."

"Oh, it's probably damaged." He swiped his bracelet a second time. "Come. I'll pay."

"Um…" she said, glancing at the train and down at her bracelet again. "It's never done this before. I don't think it's damaged."

"You can investigate further on the train," he said, pulling her into one of the middle cars.

"I've got more than enough credits. So that can't be it."

"It's damaged," he said as the train floated away from the platform. It carried more people away from Rosedel in the evening than in the morning. These people worked in the expensive city during the day and commuted home in the evenings.

"These bracelets are almost indestructible." She sighed as she gave up trying to troubleshoot the bracelet. "I don't think it's broken, but I don't know what's wrong, either." She surveyed the commuters traveling with her. "I bet Rosedel is one of only a handful of districts that employ so many people."

"I wonder why they work in Rosedel," he said in a lowered voice. "If they needed credits, they'd earn more working in Lunar City or Anteros."

"Maybe family obligations," she said, matching Brian's quiet voice.

Thirty minutes later, Cora and Brian stepped off the train into a light drizzle. The Weather Bureau dissipated storms, lowered or raised temperatures to prevent crop damage, and managed precipitation by allowing it to fall after sunset. However, it could occur at any time during the evening. They always published their schedule ahead of time, but Cora usually forgot to check.

Her curls separated into shoulder-length dark brown ringlets as her clothes became damp. She trudged from the train and onto a busy street, hoping to find a hired transport. But her bracelet still wouldn't work. The buttons remained unresponsive, and she couldn't activate a floating screen.

"Still not working?" Brian asked as he fell in step beside her.

"Can't figure out what's wrong." Cora tried again to activate her bracelet.

"Let me." He activated his bracelet, calling an automated transport. It arrived in less than a minute, and he pulled her into the waiting car. LARA, the city's AI, controlled these transports as well. They hovered a meter off the ground and wound their way to a traveler's destination.

When the transport stopped at Cora's family home, they both leaped out and hurried to the front door. Cora nearly collided with it as she expected it to slide open. She banged on the door as her irritation rose. Brian waved his bracelet in front of the door.

"May I help you, Brian Farris?" Haley, the house's AI, asked.

"Haley, open the door," Brian said.

"My sensors detect Coraline Brimble, but not her bracelet. Did it malfunction?" Haley asked.

Brian nodded. "Yes, it's broken. Would you let us in—we're getting wet?"

"Welcome home, Coraline. Welcome, Mr. Farris." Haley said as the door swung open.

Cora and Brian dove into the foyer and the door glided closed behind them. Warm air filled the entryway, helping to dry and warm them. After a few moments, she relaxed with the warmth and lowered her shield as she began to feel normal again.

"Evening, you two. Where did you go this afternoon?" Aunt Ferna breezed into the entrance hall.

"Aunt. It's a wet, cold evening," Cora said as a greeting.

"I know. I read about it this morning." Aunt Ferna peered at them. "I suppose you two didn't check the weather for the day before leaving the house?"

"No." Brian shook out his hair. "It didn't cross my mind, unfortunately."

"Hmm? Well, never mind. Have you eaten?" Aunt Ferna asked. "Why don't you stay for dinner, and you can tell me about your afternoon?"

Brian opened his mouth to reply when they heard banging at the front door.

"How rude!" Aunt Ferna scowled. Cora gaped at her aunt's outburst. "Who is it?"

"Earth Global Security is at the front door. Should I let them in?" Haley asked in a cool, unemotional tone which contrasted with Cora's panicked tightening chest.

"What do they want?" Aunt Ferna wrung her hands, all her bravado gone.

"I suppose we should find out." Cora took a deep breath and forced her shoulders to relax, despite sensing Aunt Ferna's increasing agitation.

"Are either of you going to let them in?" Brian asked with furrowed eyebrows.

"Open the door, Haley," Cora said with her back straight and her head held high.

Cora shivered as a blast of cold air preceded an EGS agent as he entered the foyer. Rain plastered his blond wavy hair to his skull. He wore a black raincoat and short boots designed for mild city weather.

"Coraline Brimble?" He asked as a greeting.

"Yes?" Cora froze, not sure what to expect. She couldn't read his emotions. Most EGS agents wore a neurowall implant that shielded their thoughts and emotions while blocking other Askovians from embedding false thoughts and emotions. Looking at Agent Lewis's cool exterior, she couldn't gauge any emotions.

"I'm Agent Lewis." He glanced from Brian to Aunt Ferna. "I feel fairly certain this is Ms. Ferna Robertson. Good evening."

Aunt Ferna nodded but said nothing.

"However, I'm not sure who you are." Agent Lewis turned to Brian.

"Brian Farris. What's this about?" He folded his arms across his chest.

"We've had a report of a hacked rental office and we'd like to talk to you about it." Agent Lewis glanced around the room. "Is there someplace we can talk?"

"No! Not without an attorney present," Brian said, furrowing his eyebrows.

Cora gaped at Brian, but she sensed waves of his broadcast fear. "Let's make an appointment with our family attorney sometime this week."

"Hacking into a database containing information about thousands of Askov families is an act of terror." Agent Lewis's mouth formed a grim line. "You can either come down to the local EGS station for questioning, or I can ask you a few questions here."

The EGS treated most crimes against Askov families significantly harsher than against normal people. This was the natural result of a larger percentage of government positions going to members of Askov families who created or altered laws to protect themselves.

"You can't question her without her attorney." Brian took a menacing step toward Agent Lewis. "You can wait outside while we call him."

"Your Askovian status won't protect you if you're a terrorist." Agent Lewis's eyes bored into Cora's. "However, it's your right as a citizen to be questioned with an attorney present. Have your attorney contact us or I'll return with armed agents."

"Like I said, our attorney will contact you," Cora said, trying to probe his mind, but it was no use. She couldn't breach his neurowall.

"Look through these documents. Your attorney will know what to do." Agent Lewis pressed a button on his bracelet, which created a screen.

"My bracelet isn't working," Cora said. "I can't check that I received the documents."

"Yes. While we're investigating the hack, we've frozen your connection to the Net. You cannot check messages, travel, or program, and you cannot access any funds." Agent Lewis set his lips in a straight line.

"What? That means you've decided she's guilty before a trial," Brian said in a loud voice.

"I suspect our attorney can easily reverse the EGS's actions until we go to court," Cora said as she perceived Brian's increasing fear radiating towards her. But something about this visit felt off. "Is that right, Agent Lewis?"

"I'm not at liberty to say," Agent Lewis said in a cool, detached voice.

"Not at liberty to say? Get out! You're not helping anything," Brian yelled at Agent Lewis.

"Brian, he's just doing his job," Cora said. "More importantly, you can't throw anyone out of my house."

Brian grumbled under his breath and stalked out of the entry hall.

"I should be going anyway." Agent Lewis turned and strode out into the rain.

Brian returned after hearing the front door whoosh closed.

"Something's going on," Cora said with knit eyebrows. "How did the EGS find out so fast?"

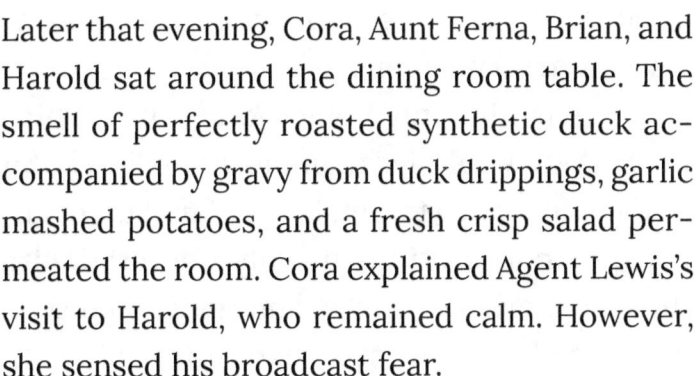

Later that evening, Cora, Aunt Ferna, Brian, and Harold sat around the dining room table. The smell of perfectly roasted synthetic duck accompanied by gravy from duck drippings, garlic mashed potatoes, and a fresh crisp salad permeated the room. Cora explained Agent Lewis's visit to Harold, who remained calm. However, she sensed his broadcast fear.

"The food is quite good, don't you think?" Aunt Ferna asked. "I'm old enough to remember when these meal crafters produced second-rate—" she gasped. "Oh, Cora, don't forget, we're going to an afternoon tea party at Mabel's. Now that you're the head of Brimble Mining, you need to get to know other mine owners and politicians."

"I think I'm going to have a headache," Cora said with a half smile.

"Very funny, dear," Aunt Ferna said in a deadpan voice and took a bite of duck. "You need to form alliances with other Askov families if we're going to keep our mine." She paused and glanced from Harold to Cora. About one hundred families owned mines in the solar system. The immense wealth created from these mines allowed entire families to become as wealthy as countries. As a result, many families became very influential in politics.

Cora's family only owned one mine, which made them wealthier than most families, but it also made them a target. Larger families, countries, or corporations usually operated with their own private armies, and they could send troops to her mine, start extracting minerals, and keep the profits. Interplanetary Security should prevent mine jumps, but the IS didn't act without the approval of wealthy mine owners. In other words, the Brimble family couldn't do anything to stop it. Right now, the Albright Corporation protected Brimble Mining. However, forming additional alliances could only help.

"The tea party's tomorrow afternoon. I'll introduce you to the Spencer family. And the McCarthys might be there."

"I already know Mabel Spencer," Cora said. "And I'm not in a hurry to see the McCarthys again."

"You know I introduced Sophia to the McCarthys," Aunt Ferna said, ignoring Cora. "It was on our last family vacation on that island." She turned to Harold. "Do you remember what it's called?"

"I didn't go," Harold said in a soft voice as he stared down at his plate.

Cora felt Harold's radiated pain. *He must be missing Sophia*, she thought.

"What I want to know is how we're going to help Cora." Aunt Ferna changed the subject again. "Should we smuggle her off-world? What about Mars?"

"Of course not," Harold said. "We'll face this together as a family. Tomorrow I'll message

Payne. He'll fix your frozen access and look into those terrorist allegations."

"I've known Zachariah Payne for years," Aunt Ferna said. "I think he'll be out of his league with this case."

"Of course, he's a family attorney," Harold said. "But he'll know who to call." He turned to Cora. "Now, girl. Tell me the truth. Did you hack into the rental office?"

She turned pink. "Um... You see... I was looking into something for a friend." She couldn't figure out how to answer. If she told the truth, she'd hurt Harold's feelings. "I promise I didn't take any information. I was just looking for something."

"Humph... Cora, I don't like this. You've the majority ownership of a mining corporation. If you go to jail for something like terrorism, the government will take away your mine."

A heaviness settled on her shoulders. "You're right. I should have thought it through."

"Cora dear, please be careful." Aunt Ferna spoke in a quiet voice. "I'm not worried about me—I already have income from my late husband. But you only have the mine, and you're supporting the cousins on your great uncle's side of the family."

Cora reached for Aunt Ferna's hand and gave it a gentle squeeze. "I'm sorry to upset you and Harold."

"What I want to know is, how did the EGS find out so soon?" Brian shifted in his seat. "Do you think they're tracking you?"

"I don't know. I've been wondering about that, too." Cora frowned.

The following day, Cora strolled through the garden at the back of the family home. In the morning sun, a colorful flower kaleidoscope, complete with subtle floral scents, surrounded her. Normally, she loved strolling among the flowers and listening to the birds, but today it felt as if a black cloud loomed as she contemplated her hack yesterday and how it'd jeopardized her family. She wore her comm bracelet even though it didn't work. However, Harold talked to Payne early this morning and thought he could at least restore her access.

As she rounded a corner, she stopped at her favorite spot and watched a bird bathing in a shallow water fountain. Her bracelet chimed, which startled the bird, causing it to fly off.

Cora grinned, "Finally."

She pressed a button to activate her bracelet, and a floating screen appeared before her. She checked her access to the Net, travel status, and funds.

"Every thing's back," Cora sighed with relief.

She found the documents from Agent Lewis and forwarded them to Payne with a thank-you note.

"Cora!" Aunt Ferna called in a sing-song voice. "You have a visitor."

"I'm by the fountain," Cora called as she turned toward the sound of her aunt's voice.

"There you are," Aunt Ferna said. "I was afraid I'd find you brooding out here, but you look good."

"I just checked my comm. Everything's working again," Cora said and turned to Brian. "How are you this morning?"

"Excellent. I'm happy to hear the attorney reversed your frozen access," Brian said.

"Yes, I found out just before you two arrived," Cora said.

"Well, if you'll excuse me, I'm going to continue my walk through the garden," Aunt Ferna swept away from the fountain and onto a shady path.

Cora and Brian waited for her to disappear into a copse of trees.

"Are you going to check on that program you left running at the rental office?" Brian asked in a low voice.

"I was waiting for it to send me a message." She glanced at her bracelet. "Nothing so far."

"I suppose the EGS has already deactivated it."

"It's possible, but I don't think so," she frowned. "I put in a lot of fail-safes so that it'd notify me in case anyone tampered with it. I think it's still running, but I can't believe it needed this much time."

"Is the database larger than expected?" he asked.

"No... I think the rental office may have better security than I expected." She sighed. "I guess we—"

Cora's bracelet chimed, interrupting her sentence. She selected a flashing circle on her floating screen, which displayed the caller. "Steven," she moaned and selected a button that started the vidcall. Steven's thin, pale face appeared on Cora's screen.

"Cora, my dear." Steven frowned. "You've been a naughty girl."

"What do you want?" Cora sighed—sometimes talking to Steven drained her.

"Morning, Brian." Steven surveyed Brian. "How's your dad? Benjamin? Right?"

"Fine. I think you should answer Cora's question," Brian said.

Steven chuckled. "I called to give you some helpful advice."

"Okay, what is it?" Cora said warily.

"You have or had a sniffer program running at Lakeside Rentals," Steven grinned. "I've disabled it and cleared the information it had gathered."

"What? Why'd you do that?" Cora shouted. "It had nothing to do with you!"

"That's not *entirely* true..." Steven's smile faltered for a moment as he glanced away from the screen. "I have a lot of clients... Very powerful clients. They pay me to keep their information safe, and I can't have you snooping around them."

"I'm not snooping!" Cora said with a raised voice. "This is a legitimate investigation. My sister Sophia spent a lot of time in that apartment, and I want to know who invited her."

"I know all about your sister," Steven said with a raised eyebrow. "She was discreet, but I still found out."

"Okay..." Cora gritted her teeth. "Can you tell me generally who owned that apartment? Politician? Business Owner? Askovian?"

"Um... No," Steven said. "Can't do that."

"Look, what I really need to know is, did the owner attend her birthday party last year?" Cora asked.

"Hmm. Who was there?" Steven asked.

"Mr. and Mrs. McCarthy, Tristan Quimby, Ruby Gibson, Brian, Harold, Sophia, and me," Cora said.

"Can't say," Steven said. "Look, if Sophia used to be *extra* friendly with someone at that table, what does it matter now? She's gone."

"Can't say," Cora replied and crossed her arms.

Steven guffawed. "Good one!"

"I can't stop my investigation. It's important." Cora spoke with a steely edge in her voice.

"Look, Cora," Steven said in a raised voice she rarely heard from him. "You already had your bracelet deactivated and funds frozen," his eyes bored into hers. "That was just the warning shot. If you don't back off, worse things will happen."

"You did that?" Cora asked, bewildered. "But, Steven, why? Why'd you—"

"There are bigger things going on here than you understand," Steven interrupted her. "I have important clients, and I have to do what they say or I'll become a target."

Steven turned to something off-screen, and Cora heard a chime, like another call.

"I have to go," Steven glared at her. "This is the only warning you'll get."

His image faded.

"What was all of that about?" Brian asked.

"Don't know," Cora said with her eyebrows knitted. "I've never seen him like that. It almost sounded as if someone forced him to do those things to me."

CHAPTER 11

The following afternoon, Cora and Aunt Ferna sat in the family's floating car across from each other. Cora wore a pale teal summer dress with a matching half jacket, which was the required 'uniform' for an Askov family afternoon tea. She'd taken the time to accessorize her jewelry and shoes.

Aunt Ferna dressed a little more formally in a full dress suit, covered in a floral pattern of large red and gold flowers and a matching green and gold hat. She'd insisted on taking Cora to introduce her to more Askov families.

Their car slowed and descended as it entered an extensive park surrounding an enormous house. The Spencer family seat included a four-teen-room home with enough sitting rooms to host a hundred or so people. The front of the home resembled a traditional manor home—essentially a large rectangle decorated with re-peating rectangular windows. Designed to present a modern and traditional blend, it exhibited subdued ornate trim over each window.

Cora shielded her mind as the car landed. She and Aunt Ferna stepped out and ambled toward the open front door.

"Ferna Robertson and Cora Brimble. Welcome to Afternoon Tea at the Spencers," the home's AI said as a greeting. "I'm Libby, and I'll be happy to help you while you're here. Enter please, and make your way to the back of the house."

Aunt Ferna grinned as they strolled inside. Cora gazed at the expansive foyer while Aunt Ferna continued through a set of open double doors. Cora hurried to catch up, and they entered the largest sunroom Cora had ever seen. It featured a large entertaining space filled with twenty or so small round tables crowded with little old ladies dressed almost identically to Aunt Ferna. Most of them wore colorful floral patterns, but a few wore colorful geometric shapes or stripes. In contrast, younger women tended to wear more subdued colors. The men wore variations of brown, gray, and taupe.

"Mabel!" Aunt Ferna exclaimed. An older, full-figured woman in a purple and green flowery dress stood and made her way to Aunt Ferna. "I've been looking forward to your tea party all week." The two women kissed on the cheek. Aunt Ferna turned to Cora. "You remember my niece?"

"Of course. How are you, Cora?" Mabel kissed Cora on the cheek. "I suppose you'd prefer a younger crowd?"

"Hello, Ms. Spencer," Cora's lips formed a small smile.

"Oh, none of that," Mabel wrinkled her nose. "It's true I haven't seen you for several years, but please call me Aunt Mabel."

"Aunt Mabel, then," Cora's shoulders relaxed.

"Now, you run off to the garden and meet the youngsters," Mabel gestured to the open folding doors that led to the garden.

Cora hesitated, wanting to talk to Mabel, but she and Aunt Ferna melted away into the party. Deciding to try later, Cora made her way to the garden and paused to gaze at the well-maintained groomed flower beds. Someone, probably Mabel, planned the entertaining spaces in the garden, so each had a little privacy and a beautiful view of one or two flower beds. Cora didn't know much about growing flowers, but the beds shaped in geometric patterns contrasted well with the flower shapes.

Trees were planted in strategic clusters throughout the garden and hosted benches and or small round tables. Guests, sipping tea and chatting, congregated around the table and chairs visible to Cora. She decided to tour the garden.

A few minutes later, she reached the edge of the tea party, found an empty table, and took a seat.

"Hello again, Cora," Libby said in a crisp, efficient voice, emanating from the meal crafter at the center of the table. "Would you like tea and raspberry jam cookies?"

Cora chuckled, "I suppose Aunt Mabel programmed you with that information?"

"Ms. Mabel likes her guests to enjoy her parties," Libby replied.

"When I was eleven, I ate loads of raspberry jam cookies. I couldn't get enough." Cora grinned.

"Oh, I didn't mean to offend you," Libby spoke in a high-pitched voice. "What would you prefer instead?"

"Actually, now that I think about it, I'd like tea and raspberry jam cookies," Cora spoke in a wistful tone. "I haven't had those cookies in years."

A moment later, hot tea with plenty of synthetic milk and sugar materialized on the table next to a plate full of cookies. Cora chortled and took a bite of a cookie. She scrunched her face and placed the rest of the cookie on the side of the plate. Reaching for her tea, she swallowed and coughed at the taste.

"Are you alright?" A woman in a pale, yellow dress asked as she approached the table.

"Yes, I was just surprised," Cora coughed again. "Water, Libby." A tall glass materialized on the table and Cora gulped.

"Something wrong with the tea?" A twenty-something woman in the yellow dress gestured to a seat opposite Cora who nodded.

"No, not really," Cora took another sip. "I used to have a huge sweet tooth. Nothing ever had enough sugar. Libby's database still has my childhood favorites. These included a high dose of sugar. I tried it, and it's too sweet."

"I'm Ivy," she said as she scanned the cookies on the plate. "Do you mind if I try one?"

"No, go ahead. But I warn you, they're sweet," Cora said.

"Mmm… I love them," Ivy said around a full mouth.

"You're welcome to them. I'm Cora, by the way." She took another sip of water.

"Cora, would you like something else instead?" Libby asked.

"No, I'll stick to water, thank you."

Cora watched Ivy happily gobbling the cookies, wondering how she could stand the sugar.

"Are you enjoying the party?" Ivy asked after eating a few cookies.

"Yes, the garden's beautiful," Cora said. "How do you know the Spencers?"

"I'm here with Reggie, Mabel Spencer's nephew." She nibbled on another cookie. "I just tagged along." She glanced back toward the house. "He'll join me in a few minutes." She turned to Cora. "How do you know the Spencers?"

"Mabel Spencer and my Aunt Ferna have been friends forever." Cora settled into her seat now that she'd washed away the sticky sweet taste of the cookie. She peeked in the house's direction and sighed. "I suppose I should mingle."

"Oh no, don't go yet," Ivy said, glancing at the house again. "I want to introduce you to Reggie. Besides, we're mingling."

Cora smiled, "So what do you do?"

"I'm a painter." Ivy nibbled on the last cookie. "I have an exhibit at the Alinac now. Have you been?"

"Not recently, but I'll make a point of it the next time I'm in the area," Cora said.

Two men walked up to their table. The first must have been Reggie, because unfortunately, Cora knew the second.

"Well, well, well," Tristan said, slurring his words. "What've we here?"

"Cora, this is Reggie," Ivy gestured to a young man close to her age. "And this is Tristan."

"We've met," Tristan stumble-sat on a chair next to Cora.

The last time she'd met Tristan, he tried to blackmail Harold and now he'd toppled into the seat next to her—drunk at an afternoon tea. She was glad she shielded herself from other people's emotions, in particular Tristan. Drunk people had far less control over their emotions.

"I think it's time for me to mingle," Cora started to stand. As soon as she slid her legs from under that table, Tristan patted one of her knees.

She paused and glared at him. "Don't you ever do that again." She stepped away from the table.

Tristan guffawed. "Where do you think you're going Sophia?" Tristan turned as if to stand but fell out of his chair.

"It's been nice meeting you," Cora nodded to Ivy and Reggie and left them at the table with Tristan on the ground. Behind her, she heard them talking.

"Who's Sophia?" Ivy asked.

"I only met her once," Reggie said.

She wondered again about the relationship Tristan had with Sophia. She found it difficult to imagine them together because she found him completely disgusting.

If Harold is right and someone killed Sophia, could it have been Tristan? She thought. She decided to investigate him further when she got home.

Cora made her way back into the house and immediately ran into Aunt Ferna. Soft hands wrapped around Cora's arm.

"There you are! I've been looking everywhere for you." Aunt Ferna steered Cora toward a group of older women at the other end of the sunroom.

Cora arrived at the periphery of the group and noticed Vivian McCarthy on her immediate right. "Oh, hello."

Vivian gazed at her for a moment. She too wore tea party attire, which comprised a flowing dress stamped with navy blue flowers accompanied by a short matching jacket. "Hello, Cora. Are you enjoying the party?"

"Yes, the gardens are beautiful." Cora surveyed Vivian for a moment—she seemed different from the last time they'd met.

"Mabel, would you tell us more about this charity you're supporting?" Vivian turned away from Cora and stepped closer to Mabel. "I think I can scrape together some funds."

"Of course, dear," Mabel said. "Quiet please." She waited a moment for the crowd's chatter to die down. "I'm supporting a new charity to save endangered wildlife at the base of our Krega Mountain range. Our goal..."

Cora turned to look at Vivian and found she'd gone. She spotted Vivian slipping back into the garden, and Cora weaved her way through the gathering to follow.

By the time she reached the door to the garden, she'd lost sight of Vivian. Glancing back at the group of women surrounding Mabel, she stepped into the garden among the younger attendees. She wandered toward a copse of trees and spotted Vivian chatting with Ivy under the shade of a tree.

"Auntie, there's nothing wrong with Reggie. He's kind and thoughtful and..." Ivy broke off, gazing at Cora. "Oh, hello again. I'm so sorry about earlier. Are you okay?"

Cora paused, confused. "Um. Yes."

"I just meant, I know Tristan was rude and I hope... you know..." Ivy's words drifted away.

"I'm okay, thank you," Cora grinned. "Are you worried I'll think badly of Reggie because of Tristan's behavior?"

"Well... I..." Ivy's face turned pink. "They're friends, and Reggie won't stay away from him."

Cora chortled. "I don't blame Reggie for Tristan's bad behavior, but I do question his choice of friends."

"And that's what I was just saying to Ivy," Vivian broke into their conversation.

"Oh, sorry. Cora, this is my Aunt Vivian," Ivy said.

"We've met, my dear," Vivian said to Ivy. "But you and I haven't finished our conversation."

"I'm sorry. I'm interrupting—" Cora said but stopped.

"No, no. You're not interrupting. I need to find Reggie," Ivy turned to Vivian. "I'll see you later Auntie." A second later, she drifted out of sight.

"Wow, she moves fast." Cora chortled.

"Especially when it comes to any discussion about that boy," Vivian frowned as she gazed in the direction Ivy had disappeared.

"I was wondering if I could ask you a few questions about Sophia."

A wary expression crossed Vivian's face. "What would you like to know?"

Cora thought of how to phrase her questions so that Vivian wouldn't disappear the way Ivy had. "How well did you know Sophia? I'm just trying to figure out if you spent time with her and, if you remember, what you discussed."

"Why're you asking?" Vivian's wary expression deepened.

"I'm trying to figure out Sophia's frame of mind before she passed. Officially, she committed suicide, and I still think that's true. But Harold's been worried about another explanation recently, and I want to put his mind at rest so he can put this all behind him."

"I see." Vivian studied Cora for a moment. "To tell you the truth, she was really Wesley's friend." She sighed. "I met her first at one of

Wesley's fundraisers. She said she wanted to meet with me to learn more about politics as it relates to mining, but she never made an appointment."

Cora considered lowering her shield to gauge Vivian's emotional state but thought the better of it. With so many people at the tea party, she could become overwhelmed by their emotions. "Did they work together on many fundraisers?"

"Work together..." Her voice trailed away, and she set her lips in a grim line. "I don't know where you're going with this, but I'm through talking. If you want more information, contact Wesley."

Vivian spun on her heel and stalked away from Cora and into the house.

Surprised, Cora stared at her retreating back, wishing she could safely read Vivian's emotions. *What is Vivian hiding*, she thought.

CHAPTER 12

The next day, Cora ambled into the lobby outside of Harold's office several minutes before their scheduled meeting. The spacious lobby featuring two walls of windows interspersed with synthetic plants that looked as if they'd arrived from the forest that morning.

"I know you need more funds, and I've already told Harold how urgent things are."

Ruby set her mouth in a grim line, facing a private floating screen. She sat at a large desk in the middle of four furniture clusters each consisting of two soft padded chairs sandwiching a low table.

"Forward this vidchat to him. I'm sure if I spoke to him, he'd understand why I need the credits now." Cora heard Oliver say.

She instinctively raised her shield in self-defense, then lowered it with a small smile—she'd overreacted.

"He knows you've lost your job and need credits for rent." Ruby took a steadying breath.

"Did you tell him they're going to kick me out of my apartment if I don't pay?" Oliver exhaled loud enough for Cora to hear. "Lunar City is not like Earth. There're more people than places to stay. If I get kicked out, I'll be homeless."

Cora raised an eyebrow at that.

"Interplanetary law prohibits evictions for a minimum of four months. You left for the moon last week." Ruby sighed and glanced at Cora.

"Who's there? I know you work in that open lobby. Who's listening to our conversation?" he asked in an accusing voice.

"Look, Oliver. I have to go. I have a meeting. You'll get the credits tomorrow, just like Harold promised." Ruby pressed a button on her comm bracelet, ending the vidchat, and the floating screen disappeared. She sighed and peered at Cora. "Sorry, you had to hear that. He was a little... panicked and difficult to deal with."

"I'm just grateful he wasn't here in person," Cora said, heading for Harold's office. "Please send him the credits. If he gets kicked out, Aunt Ferna will insist on him living in our house."

Ruby chuckled. "Don't worry, there's no chance of that happening." She stood and followed Cora to Harold's office.

As Cora entered, she gazed at her favorite feature, the wall of windows overlooking the park. She felt her shoulders relaxing as she plopped on one of the comfortable office chairs facing Harold's desk.

He grinned. "I just received a present from one of my clients." He stuck his hand in a black, expensive bag with gold lettering. When he pulled his hand out, he held a glittery orange-red ball. "This is candy from the salt mines on Mars."

"Ah, your favorite," Ruby said as she took her seat. "Do they want something?"

"Now, don't be cynical, Ruby." He surveyed the glittery ball. "Even our small mine owners deserve our very best attention." He turned to Ruby and Cora. "Would you like one?"

Cora and Ruby shook their heads.

"How do they taste?" Cora grinned as she sensed Harold's giddiness. He popped one of the treats into his mouth.

"It's such a complex flavor, salt, sugar, and something sharp or tangy," He sighed with satisfaction as he leaned back in his seat.

"I think Cora has someplace to be later today." Ruby crossed her legs and pressed a button to activate a floating screen as she prepared to take notes.

"Oh, yes, of course." Harold crunched on the tangy treat. "I know you've done some investigation. What've you discovered so far?"

"I started with Etta—"

"Sorry to interrupt, but I'm not using her in my plan," Harold stuck his hand in his bag and pulled out another orange-red sweet.

"I know. I wondered... If someone did murder Sophia, would the murderer use Etta as a distraction?" Cora scratched her head.

"I've known Etta all her life. She's harmless... Sort of... She operates just this side of the law."

"I think that's what's bothering me. She's the sort of person who can be bought off." Cora sat up in her chair to make her point.

"Okay, what did you discover about her?" Harold munched on his treat.

"I spoke to Ms. Vallencott and Omar Washington," Cora said, leaning forward as she told them what she'd discovered about their relationships with Etta, and how the Spencers had been tidying up Etta's messes.

"I don't see how this is connected to Sophia's murder," Ruby gazed at Cora.

Sometimes Cora wished she could read Ruby's emotions because her usual placid and calm exterior didn't reveal a thing.

"Etta showed up out of the blue with a strange story of Sophia being murdered. Since she's not a real Seer, and she has no reason to do that for herself, someone must've put her up to it. Based on my talks with Vallencott and Washington, Etta is not too bothered by legalities." Cora settled back in her chair.

"You think there could be ties between Etta and the real killer?" Harold stopped crunching for a moment. "I still don't think so. She just needed extra credits as usual, and usually shows up with some sort of fake vision."

"Okay, what about Tristan? Yesterday, I ran into him drunk at a tea party." Cora repressed a shiver.

"That man gets worse every year," Ruby shook her head.

"I couldn't talk to him in that state, and I wouldn't be sad if I never saw him again, but he doesn't strike me as a murderer," Cora said. "He doesn't have anything to gain from her death. In fact, as we found out, he has lost credits, since Sophia wasn't around to buy his paintings."

Harold and Ruby nodded.

"I also ran into Vivian McCarthy." Cora continued, shifting in her seat. "I tried to ask her questions about how she and her husband met Sophia but, she didn't say anything we don't already know."

She could've added that when her questions became too pointed, Vivian almost ran away, but she wasn't ready to share that yet.

"So, what's your conclusion so far?" Harold examined another glittery ball but didn't eat it.

"I don't know enough to decide whether or not someone killed Sophia. I still think she ended her life." Cora thought of the messages between Sophia and 'D,' but she didn't say anything aloud.

"I hope you're right. I'd rather not think of the type of person who could kill my wife and then act as if nothing happened afterwards." He popped the glittery ball into his mouth and chewed. "I just have this nagging feeling someone murdered her."

Cora felt the waves of his despair wash over her. Sure that Sophia took her own life, Cora hoped he'd feel better with time.

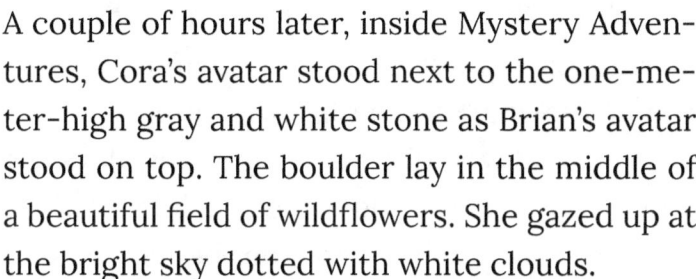

A couple of hours later, inside Mystery Adventures, Cora's avatar stood next to the one-meter-high gray and white stone as Brian's avatar stood on top. The boulder lay in the middle of a beautiful field of wildflowers. She gazed up at the bright sky dotted with white clouds.

"Admiring your own work?" Brian's avatar asked in a mildly irritable voice.

"Actually, yes," Cora's avatar chuckled as she watched him struggle to decipher the puzzle over the boulder. "Do you want me to give you a hint?"

"No, I can figure it out for myself." He made a quarter turn. "I know it has something to do with this imaginary step, but I can't figure out what to do next." He hopped into the air and landed on a step that appeared out of nowhere. A moment later, he tumbled to the ground.

Cora stepped around the rock and gave Brian a hand to help him stand. She giggled.

"I'm glad you're enjoying yourself. You realize this boulder puzzle will be too difficult for most people," he said, folding his arms and glaring at her.

She chuckled. "I'm sorry, I shouldn't laugh. You're right. There's not enough information in the clue." She walked slowly around the large stone. "How about 'Stand on top and step *onto* the unknown.'" She emphasized *onto*.

"Well, that would've helped me a few days ago when I didn't know about the invisible step." He grinned. "Okay, what would be the next clue?"

"Obviously, 'Time to step into the out.' " Steven's avatar appeared beside Cora's. "I can't believe you're still struggling with this." He chortled as he scrambled onto the boulder and took the same first step as Brian. However, he pounded up the steps, which appeared beneath his feet with each stomp. A few seconds later, a shiny outline of a door appeared, and Steven disappeared.

"You've got to step into the out quickly," Steven yelled as the outline faded.

"Sometimes I really hate that guy," Brian frowned.

Cora guffawed. "He was trying to help."

"No, he was trying to prove he's smarter than me." He sighed and leaped onto the rock. He retraced his first step, but this time loped up each step, which materialized under each foot. A moment later, he disappeared, too.

She jumped when someone tapped her on the shoulder.

"Steven! How did you — You've been hacking my game again." She placed both hands on her hips.

"No, no. Nothing like that." He chortled. "I studied the location of all portals and now I can easily zip around your world."

"Oh, well, I suppose I'm flattered you'd take my game seriously enough to study it." She turned back to the sign floating above the stone. "Let me add more words before I forget. Emma?"

"Yes, Cora?" Emma, Mystery Adventure's AI, spoke in a level voice.

"Would you add the following words 'Stand on top and step *onto* the unknown' before the current instructions?"

A second later, the updated instructions floated over the boulder.

"Thanks, Emma." Cora turned from the stone to Steven. "What do you think of the rest of the world?"

"I've thoroughly enjoyed playing it, but I regret having to agree with Brian." He frowned.

"Oh? About what?" She turned and began walking to the nearest portal.

"It's a bit too difficult for the average player," he said, glancing at her. "It's easy to fix. You just need a few more instructions—just like the ones you created over the boulder."

She frowned. "I was afraid of that. I've got a lot of changes to make."

"One more thing." Steven paused and studied the ground. "*Be careful.*"

"Careful about what?" She turned and studied Steven, which was a much more accurate rendering of his face than hers was of her own. The heavy bags under his eyes and stooped shoulders made her wonder.

"I don't know... For weeks now I've had a bad feeling you're in danger, but I can't figure out why." He grimaced. "Sometimes I think I'm losing my mind."

"The last time we spoke, you warned me about disturbing your clients. Now, you wonder about your mental state. Steven, what's going on?" She asked as she peered into bloodshot eyes.

"I don't know..." He sighed. "Nothing has felt right this whole year. I..." His voice trailed away while she waited.

"Ha! I made it to level two," Brian said with a triumphant grin as he stepped out of the portal.

Cora and Steven turned to him with frowns.

"Is something wrong?" Brian asked in a lower voice.

"No, nothing's wrong," Steven said after a moment. "I'm glad you finally caught up to me. I'll see you on level three."

Steven grinned and vanished into the portal.

"What was that about?" Brian asked.

"Another odd encounter." She turned to face him. "Steven warned me to be careful but didn't say why."

"You think he's up to something?" He asked.

"No." She stared at the closed portal. "I think he's in trouble."

"Then why warn you to be careful?"

"I don't know..." She frowned. "Something's off, but I don't know what the problem is."

CHAPTER 13

The following evening, Cora stood in front of an eflector which created a three-dimensional hologram of her body. Finishing preparations for Sophia's commemorative dinner, she surveyed her image for one final check with a small smile. She wore a fashionable dress made of faux silk with an open back. It was a pale shade of gray, lasered with a subtle floral design that shimmered in the light with matching gray sandals. Her diamond earrings matched the stones sown along the edge of her purse. The dark gray colors complimented her dark brown curly hair, which was tied up in a chignon.

She turned at a quiet knock on her door. "Open, Haley."

The door slid open, and Aunt Ferna gasped. "My dear, you look wonderful! You remind me so much of your mother."

Cora groaned and rolled her eyes.

"You and your mom don't have the same personality, but you do look alike," Aunt Ferna said with a soft smile. "Nobody knows better than me how... difficult Dahlia could be. My sister wasn't exactly sympathetic to those of us with no abilities."

"I'm sorry, I forgot." Cora detected that hint of sadness Aunt Ferna often broadcast when she thought of her own childhood. She turned and faced the eflector, examining her dress. "I just want to make it through the evening without anything bad happening."

"Don't worry. I had a good omen—Oliver called me out of the blue all the way from Lunar City earlier. He's such a dear boy," Aunt Ferna said with a wistful smile. "He's come into a few credits and wants to pay me back, but I told him to save them."

Cora resisted the urge to tell her Harold sent him additional funds—he hadn't just 'come into a few credits,' and in fact had lost his job. Again.

"Now I see you looking simply stunning," she turned Cora left and right to examine her. "I guarantee nothing bad will happen tonight."

"I'm a little nervous," Cora said.

"You may not feel comfortable with everyone yet, but that will change with time," Aunt Ferna said. "This is just Harold's way of making sure you're meeting the right people to help with the mine. The McCarthys will be there, of course."

Cora sighed. "I suppose Harold is downstairs?"

"Yes, that's why I'm here," Aunt Ferna said. "Are you ready?"

"Aunt, why don't you come with us?" Cora asked, even though she knew Aunt Ferna's answer.

"Oh, no, Cora." Aunt Ferna patted Cora's hand. "I know Harold has something planned for everyone at the table, and I'd only be in the way. Brimble Mining depends on you now, dear." With a gentle tug of Cora's arm, Ferna pulled Cora through the door and down the hall to the antigrav lift.

A heavy feeling settled on Cora's shoulders.

Half an hour later, Cora and Harold walked into the lobby of the restaurant at the top of one of the Carnation Towers, which were a collection of three towers clustered together in downtown Tymal. The restaurant had its own name, but everyone called it the Carnation, anyway. Harold had managed to book a table in less than three weeks, which meant he owed someone, or someone had paid him back a favor. Cora wondered who they could be when they rounded the corner and spotted Ruby.

Cora shielded herself from other people's emotions when they first landed on the roof, but now she wished she could sense Ruby's emotions. Ruby's broad grin and inviting gestures completely conflicted with her demeanor in the office.

"Cora, I love your dress," Ruby gave Cora a warm, comforting hug. She wore a pale lavender flowing mid-length dress with long sleeves. Turning to Harold, she hugged him as well. Harold turned a little pink and cleared his throat.

"Your dress is beautiful, too," Cora said as a greeting.

"Yes, lovely." Harold's eyes darted between Ruby and the lobby.

"Do you have a reservation?" A small floating robot asked as it entered the lobby.

"Yes, I made the reservation for Harold Albright," Ruby replied with a broad smile, eyeing Harold with some satisfaction.

Cora surveyed Ruby—it had been months since she'd seen her this way.

"Please, follow me," the small robot said as it glided into the premier restaurant.

The weight on Cora's shoulders intensified as she walked through the entryway.

The large circular room contained floor-to-ceiling windows nearly three-hundred-sixty degrees around the room, displaying a magnificent view of the city. Recessed lighting lit the center of the room, which showcased a band playing quiet background music on a platform sunken into the floor. A raised circular platform encircled the band, and a smattering of couples swayed in time to the music. Above the dance floor, the dining area rotated a full three-hundred-sixty degrees per hour, allowing all diners to have a view of the city and the distant Krega Mountains as they ate.

"Watch your step," the robot glided onto the moving dining platform.

Cora easily stepped onto the dining platform because of its slow motion and the fact that it was level with the lobby. She followed Harold and Ruby to an elegant table and took her seat. Every place setting contained a name card, and hers rested between Harold and Tristan. She wrinkled her nose.

"Is there a problem?" Harold asked.

"I'm next to Tristan," Cora groaned. "He was awful at the tea party a few days ago."

"Was he drunk?" Harold asked.

"Of course."

"Don't worry. It's Ruby's job to keep him occupied," Harold smirked. "She knows how to handle him."

Ruby chuckled. "The last time he got out of line, I dumped water on his head."

"It caused quite a scene," Harold chortled.

"Really? I feel safer already." A smile formed on Cora's lips.

"Hallo Harold," Wesley McCarthy strolled to the table.

"Good evening," Vivian McCarthy followed, wearing an expensive-looking long pink faux silk gown that perfectly complimented her figure.

"Good evening to you both," Cora said.

"So, who're we waiting for?" Wesley asked, settling into his seat between Ruby and Vivian.

"Tristan and Brian," Harold swiped his bracelet over the table. "They always have the best wine selections here." A small floating screen appeared over the table near him. He began examining the wine list at the top of the menu. Soon, everyone swiped their bracelet over the table to view their own menu.

"Who's the third place setting for?" Vivian asked while glancing at the card next to Harold.

"I had a place set to honor Sophia. It's her commemorative dinner," Harold spoke in a forced jovial tone. He returned to perusing the menu and didn't notice the silence that settled on the table. Cora's eyes darted to everyone at the table while the McCarthys exchanged a glance. Even Ruby kept her head down as she continued to study the menu.

"Hallo, Hallo," Tristan said as he approached the table with a large grin.

Cora frowned and didn't greet him.

"So, where am I seated?" Tristan asked, searching the table. "Excellent. Between two beautiful women."

"Two women who know how to defend themselves," Ruby said with an arched eyebrow.

"Of course... Of course," Tristan took his seat and pretended to be absorbed with his menu.

Brian rushed in a moment later. "I'm so sorry I'm late." He nodded to everyone at the table. Walking to the first place setting. "Sophia?"

"Have a seat," Harold smiled and gestured to the second place setting. "We're about to order wine."

Everyone ordered food and wine directly on the menu, and shortly after, a floating robot arrived with everyone's wine.

Once it was distributed, Harold stood.

"I know some of you didn't want to be here, but I felt this was the best way to remember Sophia Albright. She was a spontaneous, versatile, and sometimes scattered wife. She loved being out and about meeting new people, and so this was the best way I could think of commemorating her life." He paused, blinking back tears.

"Uncle, maybe we should continue after we eat," Brian stood and placed a hand on Harold's shoulder.

"No, my boy. It's alright," Harold said. "Sophia was the love of my life. She brought me immeasurable happiness and stuck by my side in good times and bad. When we married, we promised to love and honor each other, and every day my faithful devoted wife made me feel cherished—I miss her so much." His voice faded on the last few words, and he cleared his throat. "To Sophia." He raised his glass and took a sip.

Everyone at the table followed his lead as each took a sip of wine.

"I'm especially grateful for the new family who came with Sophia." Harold turned to Cora and raised his glass.

Cora turned pink as all eyes fell on her. She nodded and raised her glass.

"I've always thought of you as my little sister," a fond smile creased Harold's face. "But you're not a little girl anymore. It's been a pleasure watching you grow up, and I look forward to many more years to come."

Now it was Cora's turn to blink back tears. A warm feeling filled her heart as she listened to Harold referred to their make-shift family. She hadn't expected such an emotional speech.

"This dinner is in remembrance of Sophia Albright," Harold regarded everyone at the table. "I want to give everyone an opportunity to say how Sophia affected their lives."

Even though the party was a sham, his dinner speech was genuine. Everyone took a sip and looked sideways at each other. Just at that moment, the band started playing a dance number. Vivian exchanged a glance with Wesley while Brian shifted uncomfortably in his seat.

"Uncle, maybe we can dance first?" Brian's mouth formed a gentle smile. "After all, Sophia loved a good party."

Harold grinned. "You know, you're right." He turned to Cora. "Would you like to dance?"

"Love to." Cora chuckled, forgetting the uncomfortable moment.

Everyone at the table got up and danced on the circular dance floor between the dining platform and the band's platform. Other diners joined from their tables and Cora grinned. She hadn't expected to have so much fun.

However, almost as soon as she started to enjoy herself, Harold started limping.

"I'm sorry, dear," Harold shouted over the music. "I think I threw my knee out."

"It's okay," Cora said as her merry feelings drained away. "I'll go with you."

She followed him back to the table.

Harold flopped onto his chair, rubbing his knee.

"I suppose I need to follow my doctor's advice and lose some weight," he chortled. "I'm sorry.

I know you were enjoying the dancing. Maybe Brian will partner with you."

Cora glanced at the dance floor. She spotted Brian's broad grin and heard Ruby's laughter as they swung each other around the dance floor.

Where was Tristan? she thought. Finding him a moment later at the bar, she groaned. His behavior deteriorated as he drank.

She turned her attention back to the dance floor.

As the music faded, many dancers drifted back to their tables. Brian, Ruby, Tristan, and the McCarthys took their seats.

Etta Johanson slid into Sophia's chair. Her white hair was up in an elegant chignon that fit in perfectly at the Carnation, but her brightly colored dress would've worked better at an afternoon tea.

"Excuse me—," Cora said, assuming Etta accidentally sat at their table.

Tristan chuckled, but she assumed he was drunk.

"What are you doing here?" Harold asked, interrupting Cora. "I know you got my message not to come to the dinner. You replied."

"Harold, I promise this is just a coincidence," Etta said coyly, turning to wave at two older women seated at another table. "Those are my cousins Mabel and Jessica."

Harold nodded to her cousins. "We're about to eat..."

"I know, and I'm sorry to interrupt." Etta turned to the rest of the table. "Evening every-one, I'm Etta." She paused and her face became serious. "I'm a Seer and..."

Vivian and Wesley chortled.

"You can't be serious," Wesley said with a condescending smile. "Nobody has that ability."

"Science doesn't recognize my Seer ability," Etta said regally, while looking down her nose at Wesley. "But I have it all the same."

"Etta, this isn't the place—" Harold coughed.

"I've had a disturbing vision about this table. This is serious!" Etta's eyes bored into Wesley and Vivian.

"I don't want to know," Tristan said with slurred words. "It won't be good." He guffawed and slapped the table.

Cora turned to Tristan and caught his quick wink at Etta.

Does he know her? she thought.

"Is this the real reason you invited us here?" Wesley asked while standing.

Harold coughed a little louder.

"Sit down, sir," Etta said in a deep, commanding voice. Even though she didn't shout, her menacing voice carried easily over the table.

Wesley took his seat again and crossed his arms.

"I didn't invite her," Harold coughed.

"It's closed-minded people like you that prevent science from progressing." Etta glared at Wesley.

Harold coughed again, but it strengthened to a hacking cough. He reached for a glass of water, but after one sip, he began sputtering. A moment later, he clutched his chest. He began to turn purple while sweat poured down his forehead.

"Harold! Harold!" Cora yelled, rising to her feet. "Someone get the medipad."

"I'll get it!" Brian raced off to the lobby.

Suddenly Harold's eyes rolled up in his head, and he keeled over onto the tabletop.

Cora heard a high-pitched scream, but it took her several seconds before she recognized Ruby's yell.

"Is there a doctor in the restaurant?" Wesley yelled. "We need help!"

Brian rushed back to their table with another formally dressed man and the medipad. Brian activated the medipad so that it unfolded into a floating flat surface while medical tools sprung to life. Together, Brian, Wesley, and the formally dressed man heaved Harold onto the platform. The automated scanners and medical tools began working on Harold.

Cora saw no difference—he wouldn't wake up. In her mind's eye, she saw Sophia on that same medipad. She saw the same scanners and tools. Somehow, she knew—Harold was gone. She saw her family fading as a tightness formed in her chest.

Now she heard loud, wracking sobs and turned. She sensed Ruby's beamed despair and realized she'd truly loved Harold, and finally she understood why Ruby had stayed with Harold all those years. Feeling compassion for Ruby, Cora tried to hug her. But she pushed Cora away, and that push triggered a memory of Sophia pushing her away.

She finally understood something for the first time—Ruby hated her, just as Sophia had hated her. And also, just as she didn't understand Sophia's hatred, she didn't understand why Ruby would feel that way about her.

In her shock, Cora's effort to shield herself fell away.

She received Ruby's radiated hatred, Tristan's panic, Wesley's terror, and the horror from the surrounding tables. She started to feel too many emotions all crowding out her feelings. She scrambled to erect her shield against other people's emotions, but she'd waited too long. The shock, fear, and hysteria from the people at nearby tables washed over Cora as she drowned in their emotions. Everything dimmed and then turned black.

Cora sat bolt upright in her bed.

The sun peeked over the horizon, and a chorus of birds announced a new day. She recognized her room but couldn't remember why she wore an evening dress. Then it all came back to her. The party, dancing, Harold...

"No!" Tears ran down her cheeks. "Harold, why didn't I believe you?"

"I don't understand your question," Haley said. "Please rephrase."

Cora wiped her face, swung her legs off the bed, and walked to the window. Even though nothing in the garden had changed since yesterday, somehow everything looked different. The happy family she'd had for the last twelve months had evaporated last night. *What are we going to do?* she thought. She gasped as a thought occurred to her.

"Haley, where's Aunt Ferna?" Cora asked.

"Ms. Ferna is in her room, awake," Haley said. "Would you like me to contact her?"

"Um... No. I'll go to her."

Cora stepped into her bathroom, showered, and changed for the day. A moment later, she stood in front of Aunt Ferna's door. Cora shifted from foot-to-foot, unsure if she should disturb her aunt.

Suddenly, the door slid open, and air whooshed over her face. Aunt Ferna had showered and put on a new dress, but she seemed to have aged ten years.

"Oh, my dear Cora," Aunt Ferna said as fresh tears trickled down her cheeks. "I was just coming to look for you." She reached for Cora's hands and gave them a gentle squeeze as she pulled her into her room.

Her Aunt's despair washed over her, but this time she could shield herself. She rarely needed to use her shield with family, but she couldn't process her own sad feelings and handle everyone else's.

"Are you okay?" Cora asked as she gave her aunt a big hug.

I can't lose you too, she thought.

"Cora? Is that you?" Brian said in a hoarse voice. He rushed toward them from Aunt Ferna's dining table and enveloping them both in a big bear hug. "I was so worried about you."

They cried together.

"Come, you two," Aunt Ferna said after their sobbing subsided. She pulled them both to a small round tall table surrounded by four high chairs. "Would you like some tea?"

She didn't wait for an answer and waved her hand over the meal crafter. Three teacups materialized on the table in an instant. Aunt Ferna handed Cora and Brian small square clothes to wipe their eyes.

Cora studied Aunt Ferna as she sipped her tea. She looked drawn and defeated, as if her sparkle had drained away. Brian still wore his rumpled clothes from last night. His bloodshot eyes and frequent fidgeting made Cora worried. She leaned over and hugged Brian.

"We'll get through this together," she said in a gentle voice.

Brian wiped his eyes again and nodded.

"How are you, child?" Aunt Ferna asked as she squeezed Cora's hand.

"I'm okay," Cora searched her aunt's face. "What about you?"

"Brian told me everything." Aunt Ferna glanced at Brian and wiped her tears. "When they brought you home, you were unconscious. Brian said it was because you're a Feeler."

"Yeah," Cora said. "I was overwhelmed."

"Dr. Ulrich surmised you lowered your shield when..." Aunt Ferna's voice trailed off.

Cora hugged her aunt who arranged her face into a weak smile.

Aunt Ferna continued, "I thought it best to send for Ulrich. He's been tending to you since you were born. Anyway, I remember Dahlia losing consciousness if somebody became upset before she was ready. You know you and your mom were more alike than you might think."

"If you say so," Cora said in a detached voice. Sophia had been her mom's favorite, and she didn't try hard to hide it.

"No, really. Sophia was more like my Oliver," Aunt Ferna said in a wistful tone. "They both always knew what they wanted and weren't afraid to take it." She sighed at the fond memory. "Of course, they could both naturally shield them-selves from other people's emotions."

"Yes, I suppose that's what mother and father admired in Sophia," Cora said as a sad note crept into her voice. She gave herself a mental shake. "What happened after I passed out?"

Brian cleared his throat, blinking back tears, and took a sip of tea. "Um... Someone called the EGS. They questioned all of us. It took forever, but they let everyone go."

"Somebody called me." Aunt Ferna continued the story. "I think it was the EGS. I sent Dr. Ulrich to the Carnation—they said you needed medical care." Aunt Ferna patted Cora's hand. "So, I also sent Nora and Ben—Brian needed help, and I thought his parents would be the best option." Nora Albright was Harold's sister and Ben's wife.

"Dr. Ulrich and Mom consulted." Brian took up the story. "They explained about you being overwhelmed. I think they gave you a sedative so that you'd sleep until morning."

"You already know Nora is also a Feeler," Aunt Ferna said. "I bet you didn't know she had to learn to shield herself from others, too."

"No, I never knew." A small smile played across Cora's face. "I could've used her help when I was little."

"We didn't know about you when you were a child," Brian said. "Also, Mom would've killed me if I'd told anyone she struggles to shield herself, even now."

"That makes sense," Aunt Ferna said. "If you're an Askovian, showing weakness can be deadly. There are plenty of predators."

Around thirty Askov families consolidated most of the wealth and power by stealing minerals from weaker, unprotected clans.

"Does the EGS know what happened?" Cora asked and took a sip of tea.

"It's too early to say, but it looks like they're leaning toward foul play," Brian sighed and leaned back in his chair. "They'll need time to look through everyone's statements, watch surveillance footage, run their simulations, and then I'm sure they'll contact us."

"I just don't understand who'd want to harm Harold." Cora ran a hand through her curly hair. "He's a tough negotiator, and I'm sure he's made plenty of people mad. But who'd be angry enough to kill him?"

"I can't imagine, dear." Aunt Ferna wiped her eyes with a small cloth.

"Maybe it's related to Sophia." Brian slouched in his chair.

"You look so tired," Cora said to change the subject. She didn't want to alarm Aunt Ferna by discussing Harold's theory.

"I've barely slept," Brian climbed to his feet. He turned to Aunt Ferna. "Thank you for the room last night."

"It was no problem, my dear," Aunt Ferna said. "And Cora is right, you need sleep."

"Yes. Now that I can see Cora has recovered, I'm going home," Brian said. He hugged Cora and Aunt Ferna.

"I'm going to get to the bottom of this," Cora said in a low voice. "I'm going to find out exactly what happened to Harold."

CHAPTER 14

Later that morning, Cora stood in the garden staring at the shallow water fountain while her mind wandered. Usually, the sound of the water calmed her, but today it didn't work. She shifted from foot to foot as her mind meandered over the tasks she should be doing. She thought of writing more code, starting her investigation into Harold's death, or helping Aunt Ferna with funeral arrangements. A deep sadness settled on her shoulders, and she couldn't decide what to do.

"Coraline Brimble?" Agent Lewis said as he approached.

His voice snapped Cora out of her thoughts, and she turned. "Hello. I didn't know you'd arrived. I'd have met you in the house." For a moment, she wondered why no one had alerted her when he'd arrived. Rubbing her wrist, she remembered leaving her comm bracelet in her room.

Agent Lewis looked younger in the sunshine. He'd dressed in a simple brown jumpsuit and his wavy blond hair shone in the sunlight. He gazed around the garden. "It's nice out here."

"Yes..." she reflected on her investigation into Harold's death. Getting information from the EGS would be a good way to start. "So, I suppose you need to question me?"

"As a matter of fact." He gestured at the nearby bench. "Would you like to stay here?"

"Sure." She ambled to the bench, wishing she could read his feelings—his neurowall concealed them.

"I'm going to need to record our conversation." He lowered himself to the bench. "Would you like an attorney for the questioning?"

"Ah... I think I'm okay." She sat upright while focusing on Agent Lewis to gather information for her own questions.

"Recording started." The computerized voice emanated from his comm bracelet.

The first questions established her identity, location, and consent. Then the real questioning began. "I'm trying to understand Harold Albright. Would you tell me about him?" He asked in a level voice.

"Um... Well... Harold was very independent and very good at business." She didn't add a kind and gentle soul. Somehow, she didn't think he would understand. "Harold created the Albright Corporation, which helped other families to manage their mines. His business made the Albright family indispensable to many powerful families."

"What I'm trying to understand is why Mr. Albright left you one of his Martian mines?"

"What?" she looked up at him suddenly. "But I'm not really related..."

"Exactly. He left one mine to you, and one to Brian Farris, his nephew."

She surveyed the water in the fountain. "I didn't know."

"You'll find out the details when his will is read," Agent Lewis said. "Do you know why he would leave a mine to you? Since his wife isn't alive, his next of kin would be his sister Nora Albright."

"Yeah, Brian's mom. I don't know why he left it to me," she said.

I'd rather have Harold instead of the mine, she thought.

"Ms. Brimble, we're confused as to why his mine didn't go to his sister," he said with an edge to his voice.

Something about his voice snapped her out of her sad thoughts and reminded her she was in the middle of an interview. The EGS was looking for a killer. She knew she was innocent but wondered if she should have had an attorney.

"How did Harold die?" she asked, turning to face Agent Lewis. "I'm his family, and I have a right to know."

He sighed and examined the path. "He died of a heart attack."

"A heart attack!" she cried. "He was a bit overweight, but still in fairly good health."

"He was forty-eight, and he'd had a few health scares," he said. "His doctor prescribed a meditab that was fitted under his skin and automatically released his medication as needed."

"Are you serious?" she asked, nonplussed.

"He never told you?" he asked.

She shook her head. "I don't understand. If he took medication, why did he die of a heart attack?" She asked in a softer voice.

"I can't discuss that with you," he said in a level voice.

"Can't or won't?" She frowned.

"Would you tell me about your day yesterday, starting from the moment you woke?" He asked, ignoring her question.

She relayed the events of the day before entering the restaurant and mentioning that Ruby seemed to be in a good mood.

"Did Ms. Gibson normally hug you or Mr. Albright?" He asked with a placid expression.

"No, Ruby is one of those self-contained people." She wondered why he asked. "She rarely even shakes hands. Um. Is that important?"

"What happened next?" He asked, ignoring her question.

She described their guests who arrived at the table.

"Did anything seem out of place?" he asked.

"No, Harold gave a speech." She paused as she tried to fight back tears. Clearing her throat, she remembered his kind words and continued. "Then we danced."

"Anything unusual about the dancing?" he asked

"No. Harold said his knee hurt, so we came back to the table, but he was fine otherwise. Eventually, everyone else returned to the table." She wrinkled her nose. "That's when we met Etta."

"Had you seen her anywhere before?" he asked.

"No. Yes. Sort of." She frowned. "What I mean is, I hadn't been introduced to her, but I knew what she looked like. Etta's a Seer, and I saw her in a copy of a conversation with Harold where she'd made a prediction. Last night, she showed up uninvited and sat in Sophia's chair—seemed disrespectful to me."

"Do you have any idea why she would sit at your table?" he asked.

"Well... I don't know where to start." She paused as she gathered her thoughts.

"Just start at the beginning." He urged.

"In Etta's vision—the one she shared with Harold in the conversation I saw—someone murdered Sophia by putting something in her drink. She said the murderer would strike again," Cora said.

"What? Why didn't he bring this to the EGS?" Agent Lewis asked with a sharpness in his voice. "If she really is a Seer, we could've increased security. If she's a fraud, then she may be responsible for his death."

"Etta is a fraud. Harold laughed when he told me about her," she sighed. "Unfortunately, Harold created a scheme to flush out Sophia's killer. Originally, he was going to use Etta, but I got him to change his mind. It all sounded dangerous to me, and I tried to get him to contact the EGS, but he refused."

"Okay, what was his 'scheme?'" he asked.

"Harold felt that the person who murdered Sophia must have been at that table a year ago." She sighed. "He decided to hold a dinner and invited everyone who'd been there last year. He planned to have Etta make up a vision that would unnerve the killer. Setting up a biometric recording of everyone at the table, he intended to review their reactions to Etta's fabricated vision." She frowned. "Like I said, I convinced him not to use her, and instead he gave an emotional speech, hoping to make the killer uncomfortable. I believe he still created a biometric recording. Did you find it?"

He pressed a button on his comm bracelet and opened a private screen. "No. We didn't know about it. We'll look for it." He entered some information on the screen and then turned his attention back to her.

"Until today, I believed Sophia took her own life." Cora said, standing and pacing to the fountain. "I went along with everything to prove Harold was wrong. Now, I wish I'd done things

differently." She turned to face him as he'd followed her. "Maybe he'd still be alive." Her eyes
filled with tears again, and she quickly wiped
them away.

"Do you have any idea who would want
Harold dead?" He spoke in a level tone.

"I don't trust Etta. There's something off
about her." She turned away from the fountain
and ambled further into the garden. This forced
him to follow and continue the conversation.
"But Etta wasn't at the table last year. It's doubt-
ful she's connected with the killer, assuming the
same person killed Sophia and Harold. What do
you know about her?" She made her way over a
winding path as a squirrel scurried past.

"This is an active investigation, and I can't
discuss it with you," he said. "After Etta sat at
the table, what happened?"

"Etta started explaining she's a Seer." She
turned and continued their walk down a shady
path. "There's no such thing, of course. But
Wesley became furious, and he and Etta exchanged words. Then Harold..." Clearing her
throat, she continued the walk in silence, trying
to rein in her sadness.

"Yes, of course," he said.

A moment later, they stepped out of the shady path and out into the sunshine. The path meandered among rectangular flower beds spaced at regular intervals.

"Do you remember anything else about the evening?" he asked.

She took a deep breath. "No, that's it."

"Now, I have a few more questions about your programming skills." He gazed at a passing bee, almost as if the question wasn't important.

Cora couldn't read his emotions, but she could still read body language. Somehow, this question was the point of the entire interview. "Well, I graduated from the Young Science Academy—" she said as she wracked her brain to understand what he really wanted.

"Actually," he said, interrupting her. "We're interested in your skill set."

"You're going to have to narrow that down," she said with a lopsided smile. "I've been programming for more than ten years." She gazed at him for a moment. "Which specific skills are you interested in?"

He sighed and examined that path again before turning to survey her. "Do you know how to program nanobots?"

She chortled. "Of course. Every first-year learns how to program basic microscopic robots. But there're thousands of different types used in manufacturing, military weapons, interplanetary communications, to name a few." She crossed her arms. "Now, why don't you tell me what this is all about? I've a degree plus twelve years of experience. I might be able to help with your investigation."

He paused for a moment. "When we examined Mr. Albright's last medical scans, we discovered the remains of robotic parts quickly dissolving in his blood. They're gone now, but we think Mr. Brian Farris was able to scan Mr. Albright faster than the murderer intended. If he had been a few minutes slower, we would've never known."

"Dissolving robotic parts?" She spoke in a quiet voice while examining the trees. "That's military grade. I don't have that kind of access." She ran both hands through her curly locks. "Those military nanobots require a higher level of programming than I can do." She began to understand where this line of questioning was going.

"Even if you can't, you must have hacker friends who can," he said.

"I suppose," she said, ignoring his reference to her friends as hackers. "But I don't see why they would want to kill my brother-in-law."

"Tell me who you think could and let me find that out."

She smirked. "I'm not giving up my friends."

"Even to save your skin?" He frowned.

"So, either I give up my friends or you'll arrest me?" she asked, taking a moment to study his words and his posture. He was trying to intimidate her. "What evidence do you have?"

"I'm not saying I'll arrest you. I'm simply gathering evidence," he said.

"Agent Lewis, have you worked against Global Network criminals before?" she asked and changed to an impassive expression to match his. She waited until he nodded before continuing. "The Network links every part of our lives, and I know people who tip-toe through the Net as easily as a child skips across grass. I don't want to antagonize them unless I'm sure they're guilty."

"So, you admit your friends are Net criminals?" He leaned toward her.

She chuckled, covering her rising panic. "I'm not admitting to anything. I'm saying I know what my friends do for a living, but we're friends for different reasons."

"You're just going to let one of your friends get away with murder?" He spoke in a sharp tone of voice.

"No." She maintained a placid face. "The best I can offer is to ask around. If I believe one of them is the murderer, I'll happily work with the EGS to bring them in."

Agent Lewis's face swung from anger to frustration and ended in contempt. "As we continue our investigation, if we find any evidence that you or any of your friends are involved, we'll arrest you." His nostrils flared. "You may be a Brimble, but you aren't above the law." He swiped a hand over his bracelet, causing the floating screen to disappear.

"Recording ended," a computerized voice said.

He turned and stomped out of the garden. Cora shivered, watching his retreating back. Thinking of his questions about inheriting Harold's mine, her programming background, and her hacker friends made her wonder if she was the main suspect.

CHAPTER 15

A few hours later, Cora sat at her desk in her room with a plan of action. She wore her bracelet and used it to create several floating screens. She'd used these screens to program a new sniffer to dig into Lakeside Rentals and target ownership of the apartment where Sophia spent so much time. This time, it'd broadcast the information right away.

"Okay... Okay..." she said, while checking her program. She took a bite of her sandwich, grinned, and launched the program. Knowing Steven, he'd have several checks on that rental that'd prompt him to contact her immediately. She took another bite of her sandwich and glanced through her window, wondering if she had time for a quick walk around the garden. She stood but paused when she heard a chime.

A new screen popped up next to her programming screens.

"Incoming call from Steven," Haley, the Brimble home's AI, said in a neutral voice. Cora grinned, swallowed her sandwich, and took her seat.

"Good afternoon, Steven," Cora said. "I didn't expect to hear from you so soon."

"Of course you expected me!" Steven yelled. "You know I can't allow you to broadcast ownership information. You nearly got me in trouble."

"I know, and I am sorry about that." She fought back a chuckle threatening to escape. "This is the fastest way I have to contact you."

"What do you want?" He spoke in a grumpy voice.

"The EGS visited me this morning." Her face grew more serious. "I'm their primary suspect, and do you know why?"

"Nanobots." He spoke in a quiet voice.

"How did you..." Cora asked and then paused. "Wait... Was that you?"

"Every first-year knows how to program nanobots." He sighed. "Anyway, I read your case file. They think you're a master criminal. The EGS is incompetent."

"These aren't just any nanobots, they're military grade," she said. "You're the only programmer I know with that kind of background."

"There're at least a hundred thousand hackers with that background," he smirked.

"And you're all linked and have formed an elite club. That means either you or someone you know coded those nanobots." She crossed her arms.

"Look, the next time you try to break into Lakeside Rentals, I'll tell the EGS about your hacking skills." He leaned forward. "And you already have enough problems."

"That's right, they're already after me. What's one more thing?" She paused and tried a new tack. "Why don't we meet? I haven't seen you in a long time."

"So you can read my emotions? No way!" Steven grimaced. "I've had enough of that already."

"What does that mean?" Cora asked. "Who else do you know who can read emotions?"

"Never mind. I'm not meeting you, and I'm going to end this call." He raised his arm as if to activate his bracelet.

Cora had to think fast. "I've an idea. I'll make a guess who's paying you and you can tell me if I'm wrong."

Steven opened his mouth to respond.

She interrupted Steven. "Now, I know you charge a lot because you're good. You also have military-grade programming experience, which someone wealthy and connected to the government would need. You're not afraid to work in the gray areas of the law, which would help someone not precisely following the rules." She covered her mouth to hide a smile because he rubbed his neck when she mentioned 'wealthy' and 'government'. "How did I do?"

"You know, I'm really quite busy," he said.

Cora smirked. "I'm going to assume the person who killed Harold and Sophia was at the table." She stood and paced to her window. The call screen followed her, and she turned to face Steven. "I struggle with motive, because Brian inherited one of Harold's mines, but he loved his uncle." Turning, she studied the peach-colored roses blooming near the entrance to the garden. "Ruby loved Harold, so she wouldn't have killed him." She paced back to her desk and took a seat. "Sophia owed Tristan credits, and Harold promised to pay him. He would've gained more by having them both alive."

"So where're you going with this?" He folded his arms.

"The only people left at the table are Wesley and Vivian McCarthy," she said with a note of triumph. "They're wealthy and connected with the government. Did Sophia have an affair with Wesley?"

"Oh, look at the time. I have to go." He raised his arm and selected a button on his bracelet to end the call.

Cora examined the blank space after his image faded. Steven didn't say she was wrong. She couldn't be one hundred percent sure, but maybe Wesley paid Steven. "How do I verify Sophia had an affair with Wesley?" She stood and paced just once about her room. "I'll have to visit them and ask. Simple!"

Swiping her hand over her bracelet, she created a new floating screen. On this screen, she created a new message to Wesley and Vivian McCarthy.

Dear Wesley and Vivian McCarthy,

Thank you so much for the flowers and your words of condolence. I hope this isn't an inconve-

nience, but I need to discuss something delicate, and I thought you might be able to help me.

Regards, Cora

Cora checked the message, grinned, and sent it.

"Ms. Ferna isn't in her room," Haley said when Cora appeared at Aunt Ferna's room door. "You'll find her in the small sitting room with Ms. Gibson."

Cora turned and headed for the antigrav lift. A moment later, she stepped into a small cozy sitting room used for close friends and family. The decor was similar to the more formal sitting room, except that it contained fewer pieces of furniture. Only one sofa, two overstuffed chairs, several side tables, and a coffee table comprised all the furniture. The walls consisted of a few family images, including Harold and Sophia, as well as Cora's mom and dad.

Aunt Ferna must have ordered tea and sandwiches. Both sat untouched on the coffee table. Sitting on the sofa, Ruby cried on Aunt Ferna's shoulder while Aunt Ferna wiped at her own tears. Cora teetered at the entrance, wondering if she should intrude.

Ruby must have loved Harold for years, and now needs a shoulder to cry on, she thought.

Aunt Ferna raised an arm and waved her in. Ruby hurriedly wiped her eyes. Cora remembered sensing Ruby's broadcast hatred when Harold died. She entered with cautious steps, even though she detected no emotions now.

"Maybe I should come back at another time." Cora spoke in a quiet voice. "I didn't mean to intrude."

"No, no... That's okay." Ruby produced a watery smile. "I didn't mean to come over here and cry."

Cora took a seat in one of the overstuffed chairs, but remembering Ruby's broadcast hatred, she couldn't relax.

"It's alright dear," Aunt Ferna wiped her tears as well. "We all miss him so much."

"I came over to see if I could help with the funeral arrangements," Ruby said.

"Well, I haven't started thinking about it," Aunt Ferna said. "I've never handled funeral arrangements. Dahlia, Cora's mom, made funeral preparations for our parents and my husband. Harold took care of Dahlia and Max,

Cora's parents. I'm not sure what happened with Sophia."

"Probably Ruby," Cora said as she tried to read Ruby's emotions again but failed. "I think she handled mom and dad's funerals as well as Sophia's."

"Oh, my dear..." Aunt Ferna said with raised eyebrows. "Well, of course, you took care of everything. You're very efficient that way."

"That's why I came by to help." A small smile crept over Ruby's face. "I've done it lots of times, and I know what to do."

"But you need time to grieve, too," Cora said, feeling sorry for Ruby despite the hatred she'd sensed earlier. "Let's hire some of it out."

"What?!" Aunt Ferna said in a raised voice.

"No!" Ruby said in a definitive tone. "I'd rather do it than allow a stranger... It'll be the last thing I do for him."

"Of course," Cora said, but their objections didn't surprise her. Aunt Ferna would want to follow tradition, and Ruby loved Harold. "Please let me know if I can help."

"Yes, I'll do that." Ruby took her first sip of tea. She grimaced and placed the teacup back on the table.

"Oh, my dear, it must be cold." Aunt Ferna selected a button on her bracelet. "Try it now."

"Perfect," she said, taking another sip. "I also came to tell you that the EGS is investigating your Ganymede mine and both of Harold's mines."

"Agent Lewis told me," Cora sighed. "It seems I'm a suspect."

"Oh no!" Aunt Ferna kneaded her hands. "We need to call Payne!"

"No, he's only a family attorney." Cora sensed Aunt Ferna's radiated fear. "We need a criminal attorney."

"What will become of us if you're arrested?" Aunt Ferna said. "We'll be penniless." Now it was Ruby's turn to pat Aunt Ferna's hand.

"Let's not jump to conclusions," Cora said, trying to calm Aunt Ferna. "We're a long way off from an arrest."

Hopefully, she thought.

The following morning, Cora made her way to breakfast. As she stepped into the dining room, a broad grin covered her face when she saw Brian and Aunt Ferna at the table.

"Brian! What're you doing here?" Cora leaned over him for a hug.

"I stopped by to check on you, but Aunt Ferna wouldn't let me leave without breakfast," Brian chuckled.

Cora leaned over her aunt for a quick hug before she took her seat. "Well, I'm glad she did. It'll give us time to catch up."

Cora's appetite had been almost non-existent since Harold's passing, and even now she wasn't hungry. She glanced at Brian, who poked his synthetic eggs while Aunt Ferna nervously nibbled on toast. She sat at the table and used the meal crafter to get a cup of coffee.

"So, have you spoken to the EGS?" Brian asked and took a sip of tea.

"Unfortunately." Cora warmed her hands against her coffee cup. "They seem to think I killed Harold."

"What?!" Brian exclaimed, sitting upright and gazing at Cora.

"Oh, I don't know what we're going to do." Aunt Ferna nibbled more toast. Fresh waves of Aunt Ferna's fear washed over Cora.

"How could they...?" Brian said.

Cora raised a hand and Brian quieted. She perceived his transmitted anger bubbling underneath his unspoken words. "When Sophia died, I inherited her mine. When Harold died—"

"You inherited one of the Martian mines," Brian slowly exhaled. "I didn't think about that."

Cora sensed the thin fingers of Brian's fear underneath his anger.

"I had the impression I'm his only suspect." Cora took a sip of coffee. "The only thing they're looking for is proof."

"You need an attorney!" Brian said in a raised voice. "I'll ask my dad. He knows everybody."

"Yes, of course," Aunt Ferna said. "Ben will take care of everything."

Cora and Brian exchanged a glance. Aunt Ferna would be calmer now that Mr. Farris handled finding an attorney.

"Thanks, Brian," Cora said. "I hope it doesn't come to that."

"Why? What do you have planned?" Brian said in a sharp tone.

"Don't do anything that will anger the EGS," Aunt Ferna said.

Cora sensed Aunt Ferna's increasing fear. "I promise I won't do anything." Cora gave her aunt a gentle smile. She hated to upset Aunt

Ferna and turned to Brian and with a small motion, shook her head.

"Good. I'm glad that's settled," Aunt Ferna said. "Not too hungry. I think I'll go back to my room."

"Of course, I'll talk to you later," Cora said.

Brian stood and hugged Aunt Ferna as she made her way out of the room.

"Okay, now what're you up to?" Brian said as soon as the door slid closed behind Aunt Ferna.

"I'm going to visit the McCarthys." Cora took another sip of coffee. "I'm going to ask Wesley if he had an affair with Sophia."

"What?!" he exclaimed. "You can't just ask!"

"Someone murdered Harold." *And took away my family*, she thought. "The EGS has decided I'm guilty and they're going to haul me off to prison," she said with an edge to her voice. "I don't have the luxury of proper etiquette."

"This is insane." He ran a hand through his hair. "I'm going with you."

"What? No!" Cora cried. "I'm going on my own!"

"You've no idea who you're dealing with." His steely eyes bored into hers. "Wesley has no problem pulling up or making up past transgressions, then parading them in public."

"I don't need to be quick on my feet." She crossed her arms. "I just need him to react."

"Okay, so he gets angry or embarrassed or something else. Then what?" he asked. "You still won't have proof!"

"Of course not! I can't get proof, but the EGS can legally investigate him." She set her mouth in a grim line. "I just need to find a reason for them to look in his direction." Leaning forward, she softened her voice. "Look, Brian, it won't work with you there. I told them I need to talk about something delicate. You know, Sophia's letters from 'D.'"

"No, Cora!" He said. "It's too dangerous. Tell the EGS and have them look into Wesley again."

"They suspect me—I don't know if they have any reason to suspect him again," she sighed. "I've some ideas based on a little digging around."

"What did you find from your digging?" Brian asked.

"I can't say. At least not now," Cora reached across the table and squeezed his hand. She could feel the fight draining from him and now he broadcast fear. "Look, I know you're scared for me, but really, I'll be just fine."

CHAPTER 16

That evening, Cora sat on a soft sage green sofa in the McCarthys' sitting room. She ruminated with a pang of the last time she'd met the McCarthys in their sitting room. Harold talked them into attending Sophia's commemorative dinner. She wished again that she'd taken Harold more seriously. This time, she didn't shield herself from their emotions. She wanted to sense the McCarthys' reactions to her questions. Cora gazed at the large coffee table between them, wondering how to start the conversation.

Wesley and Vivian sat opposite, dressed as if they were heading out to an event.

"Our deepest condolences on your loss," Vivian said with a gentle smile. She wore a pale peach faux silk gown flowing to her ankles.

"Please let us know if we can help with anything."

"Thank you," Cora said. "Ruby is handling the funeral arrangements."

"Surely that's too much for one person?" Vivian asked. "My assistant volunteered to help her. I believe she knows Ruby."

"I think you're right," Cora frowned. "However, Ruby's determined to do everything herself."

A heavy silence settled over the room while Cora decided on her first question.

"My deepest apologies," Wesley said. He wore a black jumpsuit similar to the one he'd worn when Harold died. "But when we replied, I mentioned I had an important charity event I couldn't miss." Wesley and Vivian exchanged a glance. "Would you mind talking to Vivian?"

"Well, before you go... Were you having an affair with my sister Sophia?" Cora didn't mean to blurt it out, but there was no good way to ask a question like that.

"What?" Wesley yelled as he leaned forward while his face turned from red to purple. "I won't have you insult me in my home. Get out!"

Cora received the full brunt of his broadcast anger with a healthy dosage of fear. Now she confirmed—he'd had an affair with Sophia.

"I found several messages between you and Sophia."

"What do you want?" Vivian asked in a level voice. She radiated calm, balanced emotions.

Cora hadn't expected this response. At the Spencer tea party, when she tried to speak to Vivian about Sophia and Wesley, Vivian had fled. Cora turned and examined her for a moment, wondering what had changed.

"Can you verify they're your messages, Wesley?" Cora asked, but she continued surveying Vivian.

"I want you to leave my house," Wesley said through clenched teeth.

"Now, Wesley," Vivian turned to Cora. "Let's have a look."

Cora swiped her hand over her bracelet, created a floating screen over the coffee table, and produced Sophia's messages.

Wesley and Vivian scanned some messages. Wesley frowned, and Vivian chuckled. "These messages are from 'D'." Vivian's mirth washed over Cora and then she understood.

"You already knew about the affair," Cora said as a statement.

"Gilly, call the EGS. Tell them it's an emergency," Vivian said with a half smile.

"What is the nature of the emergency?" Gilly asked in a detached voice.

"Wait! Why're you calling the EGS?" Cora asked as she stood. Wesley and Vivian stood with her. "I'm not the one who's done anything wrong." She pointed at Wesley. "You had an affair with my sister."

"And how exactly are you going to prove it?" Vivian broadcast her glee. "Gilly, tell them we have an intruder."

"Yes, Ms. Vivian," Gilly said. "An officer will be here in three to four minutes."

"Thank you, Gilly," Vivian said, beaming. "Cora dear, I happen to know those messages are untraceable."

"Don't say anything, Vivian." Wesley turned white with fear.

Cora took a moment to think through what she'd just heard. "Steven!"

"It doesn't matter. She still can't prove anything." Vivian chortled.

Cora gaped at Vivian. She hadn't expected such a calm reaction but had thought she'd need to brace herself from a storm of negative emotions.

"Earth Global Security is at the front door," Gilly said.

"Send them in." Vivian didn't bother to hide the merriment in her voice.

A uniformed security officer stalked through the door. He wore the standard blue jumpsuit of traditional security officers. "Officer Yates. What is the emergency?"

"Officer, I'm Vivian McCarthy and this is my husband, Wesley," Vivian spoke as amusement laced her voice.

Cora probed for his emotions but perceived none. He wore a neurowall.

"This is Coraline Brimble." Vivian broadcast increasing hilarity. "She's trying to blackmail us for credits." She turned a serious face to Officer Yates. "We've known her for years and didn't want to cause any problems for her family, but she simply won't leave."

"What?" Cora cried as a sinking feeling formed in the pit of her stomach. "That's not true—I don't need your credits."

"What're you doing here, Ma'am?" Officer Yates asked.

"Blackmail is against the law. Right?" Vivian asked.

"Yes, Ma'am. Excuse me, Ms. Brimble," Officer Yates asked. "What're you doing here?"

"Well... I... It's hard to know where to start." Cora ran a hand through her locks. She struggled to organize her confused thoughts.

"Why don't you start at the beginning?" Agent Lewis spoke as he strolled through the door. Unlike Officer Yates's blue uniform, he wore a higher-quality brown jumpsuit.

"Sir?" Officer Yates asked.

Agent Lewis turned to Officer Yates. "I'll take it from here." He pivoted to face Cora. "Well?"

Cora felt half-blind—she couldn't read his emotions either.

"Um... this has to do with the death of my sister." She paused and gathered her thoughts. Somehow, everything kept spinning out of control. "You see—"

"Just a moment," Wesley interrupted her. "I'm already late for a charity function. Would you question her at a local EGS station?"

"We'll need a statement before you go," Agent Lewis said. "Where can we talk privately?"

"My office." Wesley strolled out of the room.

Agent Lewis turned to Officer Yates. "Keep them both here and don't let them talk to each other." He followed Wesley out of the room. Several minutes later, Agent Lewis asked Vivian to join him.

Eventually, Vivian and Agent Lewis ambled through the sitting-room door.

"Where's Wesley?" Cora asked as a heavy feeling settled on her shoulders.

"I don't believe that's any of your business." A mischievous smile played across Vivian's lips.

"Councilor, can you wait a little longer while I interview Ms. Brimble?" Agent Lewis asked.

"I'm so sorry," Vivian frowned, but Cora sensed her transmitted glee. "But I'm already forty-five minutes late."

"Thank you for waiting as long as you did," Agent Lewis replied. He turned to Cora. "You'll have to come with me to the local station."

"I don't understand. I haven't done anything wrong." Cora crossed her arms. "What if I refuse?"

"I'll arrest you for obstruction of justice," Agent Lewis said with an edge to his voice.

Cora huffed and stormed out of the room, down the hall, and outside to the front lawn. A moment later, Officer Yates loped to her side.

"Agent Lewis asked me to wait with you," Officer Yates said. "He should be just a moment."

Fifteen minutes later, Cora sat at a table oppo-site Agent Lewis. The room at the EGS's local station had no windows, and it was small, with dark gray walls she knew were embedded with hidden surveillance.

Agent Lewis started a recording, established the date and time as well as who was present and the nature of the complaint, and settled his gaze on Cora.

"Now, Ms. Brimble, suppose you tell me what happened?"

Cora explained about the McCarthys agree-ing to meet her because she had a few ques-tions. She only asked one question when Vivian called the EGS and lied about the blackmail.

"What was your question?" he asked.

"If Wesley'd had an affair with my sister Sophia." She crossed her arms. "I can't believe she lied."

"No, she didn't lie," he said. "So far, everything you've told me is fairly close to their state-ments."

"What? Then why did you bring me here?"

"I think you have information that may help our investigation into your sister and Harold Albright's deaths," he said. "Also, I didn't want Councilor McCarthy to hear us talking."

"You could've sent a message," she said in an irritable voice.

"I was going to," he said. "But the EGS AI alerted me when your name came up in Councilor McCarthy's complaint."

"Okay, what'd you like to know?" she sighed.

"Would you send me a copy of Mr. Albright's recording about Etta Johanson's prediction?" Agent Lewis asked.

Cora swiped a hand over her bracelet. A floating screen appeared, and she sent the video to Agent Lewis.

He watched Harold's recording on his floating screen. "This is clearly a hoax."

"But a dangerous one. I still think someone sent her. It's possible she helped the killer," she said, leaning forward.

"No one sent her. Instead, she sent herself." He pointed to his floating screen. "Needed credits. We've known of Ms. Johanson for years."

"Harold gave her a few credits. Basically an advance on her income. He did so a few times a year," she said. "But her timing is suspicious."

"I don't agree." He moved the floating screen to the side. "On another note, Professor McCarthy mentioned something about proof of his affair."

"Oh, yes." She swiped a hand over her bracelet again and sent the messages to him.

Agent Lewis took a few minutes to read through them and frowned. "I've seen these before. I examined these when your sister died. This isn't really proof."

"Not by itself. I did some research a few days ago." A small smile settled on her lips. "I discovered the Professor is Wesley Digby McCarthy. I was going to ask him if he ever went by that name."

"And you thought he'd just give you an honest answer?" He smirked. "Do you have any messages with the name 'Digby?'"

"Well... No," she said in a low voice. "But I'm sure I'm right."

"So let me guess," he said in a derisive tone of voice. "Professor McCarthy killed your sister to cover up his affair. Then he killed Mr. Albright to prevent his exposure." He chuckled. "Is that right?"

Cora's face grew warm. "Yes."

"First, when we found these messages, we questioned both Mr. Albright and Councilor McCarthy. Mr. Albright knew nothing of the messages and in fact refused to acknowledge they pointed to a possible affair. He felt Sophia was simply being dramatic."

"Yes. He never wanted to talk about it," Cora said, worrying her lower lip.

"Second, Councilor McCarthy already knew about Ms. Albright and Mr. McCarthy's affair. Although she knew nothing of the messages, they were consistent with what she knew," he said.

"Wasn't she upset?" Cora asked.

"No," he said, shaking his head. "She seemed unconcerned."

Cora reflected on her encounter with Vivian in the sitting room. She appeared calm on the outside, but raging on the inside. *Definitely disturbed*, she thought.

"Third, the affair ended several weeks before your sister died," he said. "This gives both Mr. Albright and Councilor McCarthy a little less of a motive."

"Either one of them could've still killed Sophia for revenge. The affair somehow led to Sophia's death." She sat upright with a frown. "I think you should look more carefully at that."

"We investigated a possible link between your sister's death and her affair with Professor McCarthy. We found Wesley innocent of any wrongdoing," he said in a quiet, steely voice. "Instead, I see a woman who wanted wealth. You killed your sister to inherit her very lucrative mine and implicated the McCarthys. Then you killed your brother-in-law to inherit a second mine."

"I didn't kill anyone. Harold may not have been blood, but he was family," she spoke in a level voice, fighting to ignore her rising panic.

"The funny thing is, this new evidence points more to you than the McCarthys," he said with a lopsided grin. "Was it your idea to link 'D' with Digby? Did you send the Seer to Mr. Albright?"

"No, of course not," she said in a barely controlled voice. "Did you find Harold's biometric recording?"

"Yes, but it had been corrupted." He peered at her. "That's something you could've done as well."

"You're not listening to me." She sighed. "It's a strange coincidence that the thing that could have pointed at the killer has been destroyed."

"You say didn't know about the messages when your sister was alive," Agent Lewis said. "But with your advanced programming skills, you could've easily created fake love messages."

"You're saying I killed Sophia, then created the fake love messages to divert suspicion?" She struggled to repress a shiver. "As much as I didn't like Sophia, I still wouldn't have killed her."

"Sophia was more powerful and better liked than you," he said. "I can easily imagine a jealous younger sister killing her beautiful, wealthy sister."

She glared at him but didn't reply. She *was* jealous of her parents' love, but she didn't care about the beauty, wealth, or power.

He chuckled, as if reading her mind. "We have enough circumstantial evidence to arrest you. You've been at the scene of two deaths. Both victims' hearts stopped suddenly. In Ms. Albright's case, we don't know what caused it. Initially, we suspected a drug. In Mr. Albright's case, we know nanobots stopped his heart. Now, we suspect Ms. Albright died the same way. We also know you can program nanobots. Ms. Coraline Brimble, you're under arrest."

Cora remained still throughout his entire speech and tried to control the dread settling in her stomach. "I would like an attorney."

"We have twenty-four hours before we have to comply." He swiped his hand over his comm bracelet, closing his floating screen and ending the recording. "You can call tomorrow."

Cora repressed a shiver, realizing no family or friends knew her whereabouts. She couldn't escape and no one could rescue her. She flashed back to her first day at boarding school, abandoned by her family and trapped at the academy. Determined not to let him upset her, she took a deep breath and prepared for an uncomfortable night.

CHAPTER 17

Cora tossed and turned through most of the night, but in the early morning hours, she finally fell into a deep sleep. A couple of hours later, at seven, a chime sounded in her cell. She continued to dream. Bright round lights fell from the sky, and as they hit the ground, they chimed. Studying the round lights, she wondered what they were.

Suddenly, someone shook her shoulder and her eyes popped open.

Where am I? she thought.

"Ms. Brimble. Wake up," said a woman in a blue uniformed jumpsuit.

Cora sat up with sluggish movements, taking in the room. She'd slept on a floating bed with the world's thinnest mattress. The four walls of her cell comprised clear plastic, but the floor and ceiling were white. Realization trickled back into her, and she remembered visiting the McCarthys and Agent Lewis's interrogation.

"What's going on?" Cora asked in a croaky voice.

"I'm Officer Morgan. Someone has paid your bail and I'm taking you to your attorney. Make sure you take all of your belongings." She turned and headed for the door to her cell.

"Who paid?" Cora asked, stiffly standing and trying to stretch her sore body before following the officer. She hadn't bothered to shield herself from the officer's emotions, but she couldn't sense any of Officer Morgan's emotions, anyway.

"Follow me," Officer Morgan said, ignoring her question.

When she reached the main lobby, she grinned.

"I've never been so happy to see you," Cora hugged Brian and received his warm radiated friendship. Somehow, that refocused her brain and made her more alert.

"Good," he smiled. "This is your attorney, Mr. Redcliffe."

"I understand you've been here all night," Mr. Redcliffe said. He was a tall, good looking man dressed in an expensive gray jumpsuit. "Even though you created a request for an attorney last night, we didn't receive it until this morning. My guess is Officer Morgan sent it when she arrived for her shift."

"Isn't that against the law?" Brian asked with a frown.

"No, the EGS has twenty-four hours to send it," Mr. Redcliffe said with a small smile. "My guess is Agent Lewis is a bit irritated with you."

"Would you mind if we headed home?" Cora asked. "I didn't sleep well last night."

Mr. Redcliffe chuckled. "That's the real reason he kept you here."

"Follow me." Brian gestured toward the exit. "We can talk more in Redcliffe's car."

Several minutes later, they all sat on a U-shaped sofa at the back of Mr. Redcliffe's floating car. As it lifted off the ground, light from the rising sun flooded through the car's circular band of windows. Cora squinted until the windows darkened, shading the sun.

"Before we reach your house, there're a few things I'd like to go over," Mr. Redcliffe said. "I've read through both of your interviews with Agent Lewis, and there're a few things I'd like to go over with you."

"Would you like some coffee?" Brian asked.

"Oh, yes. I should've offered you coffee," Mr. Redcliffe said.

Cora pressed a few buttons on the meal crafter's screen, and a second later, hot coffee materialized on the table. She cradled the cup while warming her hands. Still too hot to drink, she blew across the top.

"What did you discuss with Agent Lewis?" Mr. Redcliffe asked.

Cora provided a summary in between sips of coffee.

"It's true the EGS knew about the affair when Ms. Albright passed away about a year ago," Mr. Redcliffe said. "Based on their investigation, they've eliminated Mr. Albright, Professor McCarthy, and Councilor McCarthy."

"So they're not looking at the McCarthys for either of the murders." Cora huffed. "But I know there's a link between the murders and Wesley. He's somehow linked to everything."

"Do you have any evidence?" Mr. Redcliffe asked.

"No. Nothing." Cora took a sip of coffee. "Is the EGS looking into that Seer?"

"Ah... Ms. Etta Johanson..." Mr. Redcliffe said while scrolling through a floating screen. "Yes.

The EGS questioned her but had no reason to suspect her."

"Did she explain why she sat at our table?" Cora asked.

"Yes. She needed more credits." Mr. Redcliffe continued scrolling on his screen. "She claims the Spencer sisters don't give her enough to live on."

A few minutes later, the car lowered to the front lawn of Cora's family home. She finished her coffee and put the empty cup in the recycling receptacle.

"My advice is to stay on your best behavior," Mr. Redcliffe said. "Agent Lewis is looking for any excuse to bring you in again."

"Yeah. I know." She rubbed her stiff neck.

"Thank you for helping Cora." Brian slid along the seat to exit the car.

"Yes, thank you." Cora stepped onto the front lawn.

A few minutes later, Cora and Brian walked through the gardens at the back of her family's mansion. This time, they didn't stop at the fountain. Instead, they continued into the shady sections with fewer flowers and more trees whose branches provided shelter from the sun.

"I think you should try to get some sleep," Brian frowned.

"I can't right now. The EGS thinks I killed Sophia and Harold, and they're not trying too hard to look anywhere else," Cora said with her lips set in a line. "I'm on my own."

"First, you aren't on your own." His mouth formed a small smile. "You've got me."

She glanced at him.

"Second, you've got the entire Farris arsenal behind you." He chuckled. "If you need a good attorney, information, escape pod..."

"Escape pod?" She chortled.

"I'm just saying you have a lot of resources. Let me know what you need."

They walked in silence for a few minutes. Cora thought through her next steps as they wound their way along a well-manicured pathway while the birds sang at the top of the trees. As they strolled out of the shady portion of the backyard and into the light, she turned to him.

"I need two things." She counted on her fingers. "More information about Etta, the so-called Seer, and Steven's location. I want to talk to him face to face."

"How can I help?" he asked.

"Tristan. I need to talk to Tristan."

"What does he have to do with Etta?"

"I don't know exactly—I had the impression he knew Etta. Do you know how to reach him?" she asked.

"Unfortunately." He rolled his eyes. "Tristan has private rooms at the club and is difficult to avoid these days. I can take you there tomorrow."

"No, I want to go today. I've a feeling we won't be able to find Etta for too much longer."

"Why? What's going on?" He asked.

"I just have a hunch," Cora said.

"The best time to reach him is at lunch," Brian said. "He usually tries to talk someone into paying for his meal."

"Okay, let me freshen up," Cora said. "I'll meet you around eleven."

A few hours later, Cora flew with Brian in his small two-seater car. She loved traveling in

Brian's car—the city flashed by with changing scenery as he chose different routes over the city.

When his car floated to the roof of the Briny Highland Club, she shielded herself from other people's emotions and stepped out of the car. The roof contained half as many cars as the last time Cora had visited.

"Where're we meeting him?" Cora asked.

"His rooms," Brian said. "He seems to think you owe him credits. He may not be too cooperative unless you hand over some."

"Yes, he mentioned something about that last time," she grimaced. "Let's see how this goes."

A moment later, they stepped into the anti-grav lift, which whisked them seven floors down. They both stepped out onto a formal opulent hall trimmed with red and gold carpet, decorated with famous artists' prints, and flanked on both sides by black doors trimmed with gold. The decor mimicked a lavish or even palatial style, but to Cora, it was garish.

Brian swiped his hand over a sensor to the right of the door.

"Who is it?" Tristan asked through the speaker.

"Brian and Cora. We're a little early," Brian said. They waited several seconds before the door slid open as air whooshed over their faces. Tristan stood in the room with a huge grin on his face.

"My dear, how lovely to see you again." Tristan reached out, kissed the back of her hand, and gently pulled her in. His rooms consisted of a small sitting room with doors to the bathroom and a bedroom. The decor couldn't have been more different from the hall. The sparse decor comprised a thinly upholstered sofa and two matching chairs arranged around a low-quality coffee table. One wall consisted only of windows, which let in a lot of light, but faced an office building. In the middle of the day, he had no privacy. He guided her to the sofa and gestured for her to sit. She remained standing and lowered her shield so that she could read him better. His glee washed over her. Startled, she gazed at him while probing his emotions.

"Hello, Tristan." She studied him as he gestured again at the sofa. "You obviously don't remember the Spencers' tea party."

"Ah... I'm afraid I don't," Tristan frowned. "I may have had too much to drink. Did I do something?"

Cora detected greed mixed with fear. "Yes." She took the seat opposite the sofa. "I'll sit here if you don't mind. We won't take up too much of your time."

Tristan lowered to the sofa and Brian took the seat next to him.

Cora hid her smile with her hand when she sensed Tristan's broadcast irritation.

"Tristan, Cora has a few questions about the night Harold passed away," Brian said.

Tristan huffed. "I'm going to be honest with you. Sophia owed me credits, and I need them. She said she'd pay me back after I bought an art piece for her. That's the main reason I showed up at her party last year. But then..."

"She passed away." Cora examined Tristan—he was telling the truth. "How many credits did she owe you?"

"Five thousand," Tristan said.

Cora detected his lie. That amount was enough to rent his rooms at the Briny for an entire year. "Are there any records of the transaction?"

"No," Tristan said. "It... It was a verbal agreement."

"All you have to do is show your provenance of the artwork," Brian said. "Then Cora can pay you." Brian glanced at Cora for a moment, and she sensed his radiated amusement. "Unless... Is the art illegal? Cora can't pay for anything like that!" Brian raised his voice, but his mouth twitched with repressed glee.

"Of course it's legal." Tristan stood and paced about the room, finally coming to a stop in front of the window. "Fine. We actually agreed to three thousand." He raised his bracelet, activated a screen, and scrolled through numerous documents. When he stopped scrolling, he waved his hand over the screen.

A moment later, Cora's bracelet chimed. She glanced at her bracelet to confirm that she'd received something from Tristan.

"That's the certificate showing the art piece and its price," he said.

"I'll send you the credits when you tell me about Etta." She surveyed him.

"Who... Oh, I hardly know her—met her for the first time at the commemorative dinner." Tristan shifted from one foot to another. Cora felt another lie plus something. Desperation?

"Tristan, I'm sure you know her, but I don't know how well." She sighed, stood, and glanced at Brian. "I'm afraid this was a waste of our time. Let's go."

"No. No! Don't go." Tristan radiated panic. He raced to Cora's side and coaxed her back to her chair. He took his seat on the sofa next to Brian. "I'll tell you what I know." He paused. "Do you promise to give me the credits?"

"Of course," Cora settled into her seat. Her eyes darted to Brian, trying to stifle a smile.

"Etta and I go back several years." Tristan ran a hand through his hair. "She used to work in a nightclub, revealing visions from the past and future of whoever would stop long enough. She somehow got Sophia's attention. Sophia possessed powerful Feeler abilities, but still, she could be quite gullible. She believed everything Etta said."

He stood again and paced to the back of his sofa.

"The two of you tricked her out of credits," Cora spoke in a calm, level voice. "How did the con work?"

Tristan sighed. "I'm not too proud of this."

Cora raised an eyebrow as she detected the truth in his words.

"Etta always predicted something good. Something the person receiving the prediction wants. Then, she'd predict something that threatened the good thing. Really, she played on emotions," Tristan spoke in a low voice. "If you pay for this or buy that, then the good thing can come true."

"How long did you run this con on her?" Cora's eyebrows knit together.

"Um... Four or Five years," Tristan scratched his neck as if a little nervous.

"Well, she never was too bright," Brian said.

Cora frowned.

"I'm sorry, Cora. Like Tristan said, she could be quite gullible."

Cora eyed Tristan. "Is that why you need credits so badly? Nobody left to steal from?"

"Um..." Tristan shifted from foot to foot.

"When Etta showed up at the table, was she planning another con?" Cora asked.

"I don't know," Tristan said. "After Sophia passed, Etta and I parted ways for a little while. We didn't like to work with the EGS paying so much attention." He paced back to his seat. "The problem is, it's been nearly a year, and I'm out of credits."

"Have you considered getting a job?" Brian asked, in a snarky tone.

"Very funny," Tristan spoke in a haughty tone of voice. "I'm an artist. I don't do menial labor."

Brian chuckled, not even trying to hide his contempt.

Cora sighed. "Back on topic. Where can we find Etta?"

"When will I get my credits?" Tristan asked with an edge to his voice.

Cora sensed his increasing panic. She raised her bracelet, created a private floating screen, and sent him the credits. A second later, Tristan's bracelet chimed, and his frantic button pressing on his bracelet caused his private screen to flicker before stabilizing. He furrowed his eyebrows, surveying the screen, and a moment later, his whole body relaxed.

"Thank you, Cora," Tristan said with a grin as genuine relief flooded his face. "Etta lives in Rosedel. This is her address."

He waved his hand, and a moment later Cora's bracelet chimed.

"Rosedel?" Brian asked. "How can she afford it?"

"I'm sure it's another con, but she wouldn't cut me in," Tristan said with a frown. "I'm not worried—I'll come up with something."

Cora didn't need to use her powers to see his worry for the future.

"Do you know how long she's been in Rosedel?" Cora asked as a thought occurred to her.

"It's recent," Tristan said. "Just a few months. Why're you asking?"

"Just curious," Cora said as she glanced at Brian. "Any questions?"

"No. We've covered everything," Brian turned to Tristan and nodded.

Cora stood. "Thank you, Tristan," she said, and left with Brian.

CHAPTER 18

Later that afternoon, Cora and Brian took the public train to Rosedel. Cora shielded her emotions before entering the train but found the connecting cars almost entirely empty. Most people would be getting ready to head back to Tymal, not head to Rosedel.

The train's ten cars sailed over the rocky terrain with antigrav supports. As usual, most people on the train dressed in well-tailored fashionable clothing. In contrast, Cora dressed in casual slacks and a pullover top. Even Brian, for once, dressed in a casual white shirt and black slacks.

"Okay, run this by me again," Brian said, snacking on a bag of choco puffs. "How is Etta involved in this?"

"I'm not sure," Cora said. "I hope she can tell us who hired her and what she was supposed to do."

"Do you think Uncle Harold hired her even though he promised not to?" Brian crunched on another puff.

"It's possible... but I don't think so. He seemed surprised when she appeared," she said. "But Tristan knew her, and they used to trick Briny Club members out of credits. I think now he's desperate, but she's up to something." She sighed and gazed out the window at the Krega mountain range. "I don't know, maybe I'm wrong."

He chewed a choco puff. "How do you plan to get her to talk?"

"I'll just ask, of course," she said with a lopsided smile. "I've a feeling she can't afford to have too much bad publicity—someone else is paying for her to stay in Rosedel."

He chortled. "Good old-fashioned blackmail."

"No, nothing that bad," she said. "I think she'll be happy to help me."

"You should have a choco puff," he said around a mouthful. "You didn't have lunch."

"Not hungry," she said. "The days before Harold passed away, keep replaying in my head.

I wonder if I missed something. Something that could have..."

"Saved his life?" Brian finished Cora's sentence as he placed the snack bag in his pocket. "You can't blame yourself. There was nothing you could do. Anyway, you're wasting brain power blaming yourself."

The train slowed to a stop at the only station for Rosedel. Stairs emerged, and Cora and Brian climbed down and strolled past the people waiting to board the train. Suddenly, Cora stopped.

"Brian look!" Cora gasped. "I think that was Steven." But, while she spoke, the crowd shifted and the face she thought she saw disappeared.

"Steven? Your hacker friend?" Brian asked. "What'd he be doing here?"

"I don't know..." she said, biting her lip. "I can't tell where he went."

They both examined the crowd entering the train. When everyone boarded, the stairs retracted, and it drifted away from the station.

"Are you sure you saw him?" Brian asked.

"Well, no." She sighed. "I also don't know what he'd be doing here, anyway. He lives in Lunar City." Cora raised her bracelet and brought up a screen. She sent a quick comm to Steven.

"I sent him a message telling him to send my credits today," she said with a lopsided grin. She closed the floating screen. "Okay, let's meet the Seer."

He chuckled. "Have you ever thought that maybe there really are Seers? I mean, I know there are a lot of con artists, but those with actual abilities could also be mixed in."

"There may be people who can divine the future or past," she said. "But what does that even mean? We have a certain destiny? We really have no control?"

"Hmm... Not sure." His eyebrows knit together. "I think it's easier to think they're all scam artists instead of pondering those hard questions."

Cora and Brian walked for ten minutes until they reached a large apartment complex. It was one of those hyper-modern buildings with a stark white facade that didn't fit with Violet Lake's lush green foliage and deep indigo water.

"Here we are." Cora examined the address on her bracelet. "It looks like she's on the fifth floor."

"So, she's renting a top-floor apartment right next to the lake," Brian said. "What type of con is this?"

Cora shrugged while waving her hand over the sensor and entered the apartment number.

"Who is it?" Etta said in a sing-song voice.

The voice sounded so different, Cora thought she'd reached the wrong apartment.

"Ah, Cora Brimble. I thought I'd see you soon. Who's with you?" Etta said.

Cora surveyed the door until she found the video sensor.

"Brian Farris," he said.

"Hello," Cora said. "We'd like to talk to you about the night Harold Albright passed."

"I've already spoken to the EGS," Etta said with an edge to her voice.

"We just have a few questions," Cora said. "I promise we won't take much of your time."

"Are you going to turn me in to the EGS?" Etta asked.

Cora and Brian exchanged a look.

"Ms. Johanson, the only thing we want to know is who killed Harold Albright," Brian said. "We're not interested in anything else you may or may not have done."

Cora and Brian waited for a moment, and then the door slid open. Soft flashing lights lit the hall, directing them to the antigrav lift and then to Etta's front door.

"Come on in," Etta called from somewhere inside the apartment when her door glided open. The smell of fresh bread wafted past Cora's nose and suddenly she remembered she'd missed lunch.

"What's that amazing smell?" Cora strolled into Etta's home. She continued down a short hall, which ended at a kitchen and dining room combination. Like the facade of the complex, Etta's home was also hyper-modern, with two parallel white countertops. The counter against the wall rested just below a large window displaying a magnificent view of Violet Lake. The second counter stood in the middle of the kitchen.

"They're cinnamon rolls," Etta said with a giggle, applying icing to a set of rolls on one of two trays. She wore a workout top and bottom and looked like someone's sweet old grandma instead of the haughty Seer at the Carnation. "I know nobody bakes anymore, but I accidentally ran into an old-fashioned cookbook, and I couldn't help myself." She turned to the meal crafter at the end of the counter and selected coffee from the screen. "Come and have a seat. I want you two to be my testers. Would you like coffee?"

"No, thanks." Cora opened her shield to read Etta's emotions.

Brian shook his head.

"Is baking complicated? How do you find the ingredients?" Cora asked, taking a chair opposite Etta. Brian sat next to her and sniffed with a huge grin.

"Yes, and it's difficult," Etta said with a grin. "It took ages for me to find something for heating. I'm using an old-fashioned camping stove." She gestured to a red scratched box sitting on the counter behind her. "Then I had to find someone to remove the backup crafter that came attached." She pulled out a stool and took a seat herself. "I had to have most of the ingredients specially made for me. These days ingredients are made for meal crafters."

Cora sensed Etta's genuine pride in creating her baking experience.

"How long have you been baking?" Brian asked while eyeing the iced roll.

"Oh... About four or five years." Etta took a sip of coffee. "I think it's ready now. Would you like a roll?"

They both nodded. Etta pulled apart three rolls dripping with icing and placed them on three small plates.

Cora cut into the soft, delectable treat with her fork. As soon as her lips closed around the pastry, her eyes rolled back into her head. "Mmm..." She swallowed. "This is better than the crafter."

"I had this at someone's afternoon tea," Brian said as he dug his fork in for another bite. "But it wasn't this good."

Etta beamed as she dug her fork into her own roll. "They've come out better than the last time I tried."

They ate in silence for a few minutes. "Would you like more?"

"No, thank you. They're delicious, but very sweet." Cora pushed her plate away. Etta placed it in the recycling receptacle.

Brian held his plate. "If you wouldn't mind."

"Of course," Etta said with a broad grin. She took his plate and added another roll. "Before you ask me any questions, I just want you to know I didn't kill Harold. I considered him a good friend. You said you're looking into his death—what would you like to know?"

Cora paused for a moment to gather her thoughts. "We've spoken to Tristan, who explained how sometimes the two of you worked together."

Etta studied a crumb on her plate as her cheeks colored. "He always was a loudmouth."

"Would you mind if I got some water?" Cora asked, her mouth dry.

"I'll get it." Etta turned to Brian, who'd just finished his second roll. "Would you like anything?"

"Water, please," Brian said, clearing his throat.

A moment later, Etta placed two glasses of water in front of Cora and Brian.

"Who paid you to show up at the Carnation?" Cora asked and took a sip of water.

"No one. It was just a coincidence." Etta wiped crumbs off the counter.

Cora sensed her first lie. She paused, wondering which question to ask next.

"What were you going to predict?" Cora asked, leaning forward on her elbows.

"Oh, that. I would've claimed that Wesley Mc-Carthy would experience a deep loss unless he confessed to a crime in his past." Etta took a sip of coffee. "It's a pretty standard con."

Cora exchanged a look with Brian, surprised by Etta's candor.

Brian shook his head. "What did you think would happen?"

"Wesley or Vivian would lose their tempers," Etta said. "It really didn't matter."

"Why didn't it matter?" Cora asked.

"My job is just to deliver messages from the cosmos." Etta examined the living room as if gathering her thoughts. "I can't control what people do with the information."

"You're lying," Cora said in an even voice. "We spoke to Ms. Vallencott and Mr. Washington. They both confirmed that you lie for credits. What were you really going to tell everyone that night?"

"You've been checking up on me," she said in a soft voice. "I already apologized to Ms. Vallencott. And I'm sorry about Omar. Things just seemed to go wrong."

"Doesn't all the lying bother you?" Brian asked.

"Look. I can't get mixed up with the EGS," Etta said. "I want to help you, but Mabel Spencer and her sisters pay for me to stay here on the condition that I don't get into trouble." Etta shifted in her seat. "They don't mind me pulling a few harmless cons, but they'll be furious if I drag the family name into another scandal."

"How're you related to the Spencer family?" Brian asked.

"I'm a distant cousin." Etta turned pink, and Cora sensed her broadcast embarrassment. "The type of cousin one would rather forget."

"Did you kill Sophia Albright?" Cora asked with an edge to her voice.

"Of course not!" Etta said haughtily. "I didn't kill Harold or Sophia, and I'm not involved in their deaths."

Etta's voice reminded Cora of the first time they met. More importantly, Etta told the truth.

"Why did you visit Harold a few weeks ago?" Cora said.

"A few weeks ago, someone paid me to visit Harold Albright and pronounce my vision," Etta glanced from Brian to Cora. "I told him I saw someone murder his wife, and that he'd catch the killer."

"Who paid you?" Cora asked, her eyebrows knit together.

"I don't know," Etta said. "It's the truth. He... or maybe she contacted me through a vidchat. I normally wouldn't have gone along with it, but they offered me a lot of credits."

Cora nodded. She perceived Etta's truth and a healthy amount of fear for the first time.

"Who was on the vidchat?" Cora asked.

"Nobody." Etta grimaced. "It was strange. They could've sent a simple message."

"There's something you're not telling us." Cora sensed deception, but it wasn't a lie.

Etta studied the countertop for a long time, Cora thought she wouldn't answer.

"A few days before Harold passed away, the same person paid me to say you killed Sophia." Etta shivered. "When they contacted me a few weeks ago, I thought it was a prank. The second time they approached me, I realized it was something serious."

"You think I killed my sister?" Cora asked with a half smile.

Etta stared into her coffee cup. "When I spoke to the EGS, I explained that someone had paid me to say you killed your sister." Etta glanced at Cora.

"But why me?" Cora asked with furrowed eyebrows.

"Maybe the EGS would've had a much stronger case if Etta had predicted you'd killed Sophia," Brian said.

Etta guffawed. "No. Absolutely not." She wiped the counter. "The EGS hates people like me. They would've assumed either I killed Harold or I helped the killer."

"Nothing's making sense." Cora rubbed her face. "Someone paid you, which means they expected you to have time to make a prediction before Harold passed," Cora sighed. "That means something went wrong."

"What went wrong?" Etta asked.

"I don't know, but I think Harold died a little too soon," Cora said in a level voice. "We know that because Etta didn't have time to deliver her speech."

"But there are tons of things that could have gone wrong." Brian huffed in frustration. "Maybe we danced too early or too late. Maybe we ordered the wrong food or drink. It could be anything..."

"True, but let's focus on what would've happened," Cora said in a steady, determined voice. "The EGS could've accused me of Harold's murder, but they wouldn't have had enough evidence to hold me. I know that because that's what's happened, anyway."

"If we follow that line, they would've accused me of either murdering Harold or as an accomplice to the murderer," Etta said, placing the remaining rolls in a clear container.

"Even if they'd accused you, there wouldn't have been enough evidence to hold you, either." Brian said.

"In any case, I never got to give my vision." Etta placed the container full of rolls into a cooling drawer below the counter. "Harold died, and I realized someone truly dangerous had manipulated everything at that table." She gazed at Cora. "It wasn't a harmless prank anymore."

"Would you send me a copy of the encrypted vid asking you to name me as Sophia's murderer?" Cora asked. "Also, include the encryption key."

Etta nodded. She clicked a button on her bracelet, bringing up a floating screen.

Cora couldn't see the contents, but a moment later, her bracelet chimed as she received the vid.

Etta frowned. "I'm sorry I helped create this mess. I just... I have a bad feeling you're in danger." Etta reached out and squeezed Cora's hand.

Cora felt Etta's honesty flowing like gentle ripples trickling over her.

Later that evening, Cora and Brian sat on the U-shaped cushioned back seat of an empty train car. She surveyed the Krega mountain range while thinking over Etta's words. Her shoulders drooped with the weight of everything.

"Are you worried?" Brian asked in a quiet voice.

"Yes," Cora frowned. "But, I'm mostly mad. Someone is actually trying to hurt me. All this time I thought Harold was exaggerating about Sophia being murdered."

"You know there's a difference," he said, with his eyebrows drawn together. "Uncle thought someone killed Sophia. He never thought you were in danger. Otherwise, he would've never involved you in his scheme."

"Oh, I see what you mean." She sat up and turned to face Brian. "Who gains by killing Sophia and Harold?"

"Uncle Harold's personal trust has already started distributing his assets." He glanced at the floor before peering at Cora again. "We both received a mine."

Cora shielded herself before she stepped onto the train. When he mentioned the mines, a cascade of emotions washed over Brian's face.

She squeezed his hand. "I miss him too. He was the kind and gentle father I always wanted."

He nodded but remained quiet for several more minutes. "Uncle had a massive business managing mines for wealthy brats." Brian chuckled, "And I'm including myself in that group."

"As I remember, you did eventually learn to manage your own alythium mine." A gentle smile flitted across her face. "I was still learning. Not sure what I'll do now."

"I'll help you," he said. "We can work together." He squeezed her hand and let go while he leaned back in his seat. "Each mine owner's contract allows them to retrieve management of their own mine, or the Albright Corporation can continue as manager. I know most won't change management teams."

"What about ownership of the Albright Corporation?" she asked.

"The corporation has a board of directors," he said. "Mostly Albright, Ferris, and Spencer family members sit on the board. That won't change. What'll change is the face of it. I don't know how they'll get more business. Uncle mostly used his personal contacts to get new clients."

"Who gains the most on the board with Harold gone?" she asked.

"Well... No one," Brian said while scratching his head. "A separate family trust holds the Albright family mine, which pays all Albrights a regular income. Uncle started the Albright Corporation to manage mines for other Askovians. Over time, as wealthier investors joined the corporation, they demanded larger shares of the company and when Uncle passed, he only owned about ten percent. He gave away his ownership for access to a long list of potential clients." He sighed. "The remaining board members who were all wealthier than Uncle will receive a portion of Uncle's ten percent. I think this line is a dead end."

"Unless we're missing something," Cora said, crossing her arms and leaning back into the cushions.

CHAPTER 19

F or the rest of the train ride, Cora tried to make sense of Etta's encrypted messages as Brian dozed beside her. She couldn't make sense of the tracking information. She'd seen this type of encryption before, but she wondered what the hacker had done to deliver a message with no origination or destination information.

Shifting on the cushioned seat, Cora almost missed the gentle bump that rocked the passenger car. She frowned and glanced at Brian, but his gentle snores told her he hadn't noticed the brief shake. She peered at the Krega mountain range back lit by moonlight, but the train continued to head in the same direction. A moment later, Cora noticed its gradual slowing.

She quickly sent a message with her comm to the train's AI but got no reply.

Grabbing Brian's shoulder, she shook it until his eyes popped open. "Wake up! Something's wrong."

Brian rubbed his eyes and surveyed the empty train car. "What're you talking about? Everything's fine."

"We're slowing," she said in a tense voice. "The rest of the train is pulling away."

"It's obviously a malfunction," he said in a groggy voice. "We just need to alert the train's AI."

"I already sent a message to LARA. Nothing happened." She stood and paced along the central aisle, peering out the windows. "No, something's wrong."

He pressed a button on his bracelet several times. "Hmm... I see what you mean. I don't think any signals are getting out."

The barren, rocky ground surrounded the lone train car, and the only light came from their car. Several minutes later, it floated to a stop.

"I wonder if we should turn the lights off in here." She paced the central aisle. "We'll be able to see someone approaching."

"Let's not panic yet," he said, examining the landscape. "This could still be a malfunction."

They studied their surroundings for a few more minutes. Cora paced while Brian changed seats.

"Someone will eventually come for us, I'm sure," he said.

"That's what bothers me," she said in a quiet voice. "This wasn't a glitch. Someone wants us here. Why?"

"I think you're overreacting," he chuckled, but his laughter didn't reach his eyes.

Suddenly, the entire train car dropped a meter to the ground with a loud rock crunching and metal scraping sound. Cora grabbed two seats to steady herself and grunted.

The fall threw Brian out of his seat, causing him to hit his head against the back of another seat. He fumbled as he pulled himself into a neighboring seat and groaned. "Okay, I believe you."

"Quiet! Someone's coming." She tilted her head to one side as she tried to sense the person approaching.

They waited several minutes.

"I don't hear anything," he said in a slow, groggy voice.

"I can feel them." She moved closer to Brian and whispered. "You okay?"

Brian nodded. "We're in danger?"

"No... Maybe... Whoever's coming is... happy," she said with her eyebrows knit.

"You mean this is a prank?" he said in a raised voice.

"No. It's serious, but..." she said and closed her eyes. "It's hard to say what's going on..." Cora turned to Brian and spotted the trickle of blood from his hair and onto his forehead. "You're bleeding. We need the train's medipad." She surveyed the passenger car and spotted the red letters 'Emergency Medipad'.

She took two steps, stopped, and faced one of the side doors. "Brian. They're here." The door slid open as fresh air blew into the train's car. Brian pulled himself off the floor to stand next to Cora.

"Hello, Cora. Brian," Steven said as he stepped into the car. "What happened to you?" He asked as he peered at Brian's bleeding forehead.

Cora recognized his pale face and brown eyes as her chest tightened with anger. "You turned off the antigrav." Cora crossed her arms. "It made the passenger car crash to the ground and injured Brian."

Steven hid a smile.

"Oh, yeah... That was me." He took a couple of steps further on the central aisle.

"I'm getting the medipad," Cora said as she continued on the car's central aisle toward Steven. He leaped back a step and leaned against a wall as Cora passed him with a glare. She struggled to pull the medipad, a white and gray egg-shaped sphere, off the wall. Activating the medipad's antigrav allowed it to float while she pushed it back toward Brian, who regained his seat. She pressed a few buttons and a floating screen materialized over the medipad. The sphere unpacked itself into a flat surface used for more serious injuries while medical tools sprung to life. Brian didn't need the bed, so the medical tools, such as a scanner, laser, and cleansing pads, extended to treat Brian's injuries.

Once satisfied that the medipad worked properly on Brian, she turned and faced Steven with her arms folded. "Why did you have to stop our train in the middle of nowhere?"

Steven took a couple of tentative steps toward Cora and Brian. "I'm really sorry. I just wanted to make a grand entrance." He turned to Cora with a lopsided grin. "You know me. I like to be the center of attention."

Cora detected Steven's strange mix of radiated elation and fear—she struggled to comprehend it. Sighing, she took a seat near Brian. "You know my message just meant let's meet in the next twenty-four hours."

"I know—I remember the code." Steven took a seat towards the front of the car. "Why did you follow me to Rosedel?"

Cora turned to Brian. "I told you I saw him!"

Brian grunted as the medipad stopped the flow of blood and began regenerating the injured skin on his scalp and forehead so that there would be no scar.

"What were you doing there, anyway?" Cora didn't bother correcting Steven's assumption that they followed him.

"None of your business," Steven said, mirroring Cora's crossed arms.

"Okay. Why did you stop our train?"

"Technically, I didn't stop the train," Steven said with a smirk. "It should arrive in downtown Tymal in a few more minutes. Then LARA will notice something missing." He chortled.

"So you may have an hour to tell us why you stopped us here," Cora said in an even voice. "Once LARA retrieves this car, I'll be happy to tell them all about you."

Steven's grin melted, and he shifted from foot to foot. "You're right, we don't have much time." He stood and nodded toward Brian. "Is he going to be okay?"

Cora glanced at the progress screen floating above the medipad and at Brian's wounds. "Yeah, it looks like he's okay."

"I'm leaving Earth. I won't even be on the Net." Steven stood and paced to the entrance at the front of the car. "Someone is trying to kill me."

"What? Wait... What did you do?" Cora asked and set her mouth in a grim line.

"Um..." Steven said and paced past the front windows of the train's car. "Not sure where to begin."

Cora sensed more fear radiating from Steven.

"Gambling keeps Lunar City, my home, profitable. It's easy to get started and very hard to stop." Steven grimaced. "A year ago, I got into trouble. I mean, more than usual. I had to do something drastic to get myself out of it." Steven ran his hand through his hair. "I basically sold my services on the open market."

"You mean to criminals?" Cora placed her hands on her hips. "You taught me everything I know about hacking. Lesson one, never go to the dark side. Remember? You said you never know how much damage will come from a little piece of code."

Steven waved a hand through the air.

"I know… I know," he exhaled as his shoulders slumped. "I work for the military—I know how dangerous things really are. Even the EGS doesn't know everything about me." He turned and faced Cora. "I work for someone, but I don't know their name. It was an easy job—I did a few slightly illegal things, but I always checked to make sure there wouldn't be too much fallout."

"Except something bad has happened." Cora leaned forward in her seat. "What is it?"

Steven dropped his head into his hands. "That's just it. I don't remember everything." He exhaled.

The medipad completed its final scan of Brian's scalp and forehead. A mechanized voice announced, "Lacerations fused. Medical treatment complete." The medipad began folding and stowing away its tools, and then it folded into the white and gray sphere. A moment later, it drifted to the front of the train's car and reattached itself to the wall.

"You okay?" Cora ran a hand through Brian's hair to check the cut on his scalp.

"I'm fine." Brian gently pulled Cora's hand out of his hair.

Steven straightened and glanced into the darkness. "The person I work for forced me to send information about your programming background, and that virus you left at Lakeside Rentals to the EGS. It was all circumstantial evidence, but the EGS arrested you, anyway. They're all idiots."

"You got me arrested?" Cora crossed her arms. "Why?"

"I just told you I didn't have a choice," Steven said, a note of desperation in his voice.

She took several steps on the central aisle toward Steven, whose eyebrows shot up to his scalp.

He held out both hands as if to signal her to stop. "Wait! Calm down. Do you remember a few days ago I asked if you were okay?"

"Um, yeah. The day I got stuck in the scanning booth. It wouldn't let me enter the building." Cora said.

"The person who hired me said they tested nanobots on you and your entire family."

"How would they get access to all of us?" she asked.

"There're millions of ways," Steven sighed. "The question was why? Later, I learned that Harold Albright passed. I think they were preparing to kill him."

"You knew that and didn't tell me?" Cora said in a raised voice.

"No, I didn't know at the time. I asked why, but they never answered." Steven dithered from foot to foot.

She sensed his increasing confusion and anxiety. "Did you program the nanobots?"

"Definitely not!" Steven said. "I would've remembered something so complicated."

"You already said you can't remember everything," Brian said. "How would you know?"

"You're not a programmer. You wouldn't understand." Steven rolled his eyes.

"This sounds like the work of a Reader with the ability to read thoughts and change them." Cora's eyebrows knit together. "I've heard of Askovians with that ability, but I've never met one."

"I think he's making the whole thing up," Brian scowled.

"No. He's not." Cora sensed Steven's jumbled emotions but couldn't understand what they meant.

Steven smirked at Brian before turning to Cora.

"My first real job was to cover up Sophia's affair. I thought all his requests would be mundane like that. Then Sophia died." He broadcast raw fear. "I think whoever hired me killed her and now Harold, too."

"But why? It doesn't make sense," Cora sighed.

"I wish I knew," Steven said. "They have very advanced programming skills. I can't find them on the Net."

"Somebody used a weak encryption on those messages between Sophia and Wesley," Cora said. "Somehow, I don't think that was you."

"No. One of those two idiots used some sort of hack encryption," Steven smirked. "But anyone who traced the messages wouldn't get beyond their love nest. I just had to make sure you didn't dig too deeply into McCarthy's affairs."

"Wesley's behind all of this?" Cora asked in a raised voice.

"No, no. Someone else gave me instructions to protect both McCarthys." Steven frowned. "That's why I disabled your sniffer. It's not the McCarthys, but someone pretty powerful."

Cora studied Steven for a moment while he broadcast a tangled mix of confusion and fright.

"Steven, talk to me. What's going on? Why does someone want to kill you?"

"I don't know. I can't think." Steven rubbed his face. "I need to get off the Net. I just wanted you to know before I disappeared."

"Can we help you?" Brian asked, dragging himself to his feet.

"No..." Steven said, examining Cora. He opened his mouth as if he wanted to say something more. "I can't—"

He turned and sped out the door and into the darkness.

"Should we go after him?" Brian swayed as he walked to the front of the car.

Cora followed close behind Brian. "He's really in trouble. I sensed his emotions. Everything was just a jumbled mess."

"He did say he's afraid for his life." Brian stood at the open door and peered into the darkness.

Cora looked out, trying to make out the Krega Mountains. "The only thing is, what he said didn't match his emotions. He didn't or couldn't tell us everything."

"Hmm..." Brian squinted into the darkness.

Cora plopped on a seat and huffed. "Brian, what's going on? Etta thinks I'm in danger. On the other hand, Steven thinks he's in danger."

"Instead, Sophia and Uncle Harold are dead, and we've no idea why." Brian leaned on the door opening and inhaled. "I love the night air."

"This morning, I thought there was a link between Sophia and Wesley." Cora rubbed her arms to warm them as the night air rolled into the car. "It turns out the link was Steven, but now I have more questions, not less."

"Maybe we can ask Steven more questions tomorrow," Brian said with a lopsided smile. "Give him time to calm down."

"I know Steven. If he doesn't want to be found, you won't find him." Cora stood and made her way to the back of the car. She rested on the U-shaped cushions.

Brian stepped away from the doorway, which allowed the door to slide closed. "I wonder how much longer we'll have to wait."

"Probably just a few more minutes," Cora said with her eyes closed.

"Do you know what you want to do next?" Brian asked.

"I've spoken to Wesley, Vivian, Tristan, Etta, and even Steven. I don't know what to do next," Cora frowned.

CHAPTER 20

T he following morning, Cora sat in Harold's office in one of two chairs facing his desk. On the other side of the desk sat Mr. Benjamin Farris, Brian's dad. She studied Mr. Farris with his head lowered over the desk as he tapped and slid his fingers while rearranging symbols she didn't recognize. Glancing at her favorite feature, the wall of windows, she took a deep breath, which usually brought her a sense of calmness, but it didn't work today. She shifted in her seat and wondered again why he'd summoned her.

Mr. Farris slowly raised his head. "Cora, I'm sorry to keep you waiting. I needed to finish this before I forgot." He waved his hand over Harold's desk, and it cleared. He gazed at Cora for a moment. "I know it's been less than a week since Harold... Well, I wanted to give you the general gist of his last wishes. The family attorney will officially read his will in two weeks, but the EGS required the details of his bequest." Mr. Farris paused. "I'm not sure how to say this, but they're using the contents to prove you murdered Harold."

"I know, Mr. Farris," Cora sighed. "They arrested me the day before yesterday and explained. I had no idea Harold had gifted a mine to me. But they didn't believe me."

"It seems Harold held lots of secrets." Mr. Farris said and chuckled. "I didn't even know he had any mines in his own name. I thought he only held ownership of the Albright Corporation." Mr. Farris cleared his throat, and Cora sensed a wave of his broadcast grief. She received a steady flow of his oppressive sadness when she first entered the room, but it increased for a moment. If he didn't control himself soon, she'd need to shield herself.

"I'm sorry," Cora said in a gentle voice. "We've both lost a kind and loving brother."

Harold was Ben's brother-in-law through his wife, Nora Albright.

Cora sat upright and continued, "It must've been difficult to go through Harold's papers and summarize them for the EGS, and now for me."

Mr. Farris dabbed at his teary eyes. "Yes, well... We must focus on this mess with the EGS. At first, I thought they were simply incompetent, but now I think they have it out for you. Cora, what can we do to help?"

"Right now, I don't know," Cora said and gazed out of the window as she observed his subsiding sorrow. "I don't think I deserve Harold's mine. I want to give it to another family member. In fact, I want to give away all of my mines."

Mr. Farris grumbled and pulled himself to his feet. He looked as if he'd aged ten years and his stiff shuffle made him appear even older. He reached the chair on the other side of Harold's desk and sat next to Cora.

"My dear, I don't have your abilities, but I know you're upset. Never make important decisions when you're this emotional. It won't go well."

"But I don't feel as if I deserve the mines. Two people died for me to get them. Doesn't seem right," she sighed. "I'd rather not have any mines and have Harold here."

"Giving away the mines won't bring back Harold," he said. "Give yourself some time."

The door slid open with a whoosh of air, and Ruby stepped into the office. The dark circles under her eyes and furtive glances at Cora and Mr. Farris made her look as if the life had drained out of her. "I'm sorry to interrupt, but the EGS seems to want more information. I don't know why they can't wait."

Cora raised an eyebrow. She rarely heard Ruby complain. "What do they want?"

"Some information about the previous owners of the Brimble mine," Ruby said. "Should I send it?"

"I wonder what they're looking for?" Cora sighed.

"They're just covering their bases. They want to make sure your attorney doesn't have a way to wiggle out of any sort of trap they're setting." Mr. Farris turned to Ruby. "Go ahead and send it. Won't matter too much one way or another."

"The EGS has a lot more resources than I have," Cora stood, paced to the window, and watched the people walking on the sidewalk next to the building. "I think my best bet is to prepare for the worst. If I own those mines when they find me guilty, they'll take ownership and sell to the highest bidder."

"Coraline Brimble! Don't for one moment consider giving up," Ruby said in a raised voice. "Harold worked his entire life for those mines and spent years managing the Brimble mine. Don't throw away all his hard work."

Cora whipped around and faced Ruby. Waves of Ruby's anger washed over Cora, who could only peer wide-eyed in surprise. She reminded herself, Ruby lost Harold, someone she loved. But she flashed to the last time she'd sensed Ruby's hatred and again wondered why.

"Ruby's right," Mr. Farris said with an edge in his voice. He pulled himself to his feet and paced to the window with Cora. "You're a member of this family, and we never give up." Mr. Farris spoke in a softer tone. "I know you're scared, and it seems everything's against you. The EGS has technology, but you have your abilities. If I had to bet, I'd stake my credits on you." He reached for Cora's hands and gave them a gentle squeeze. "You know, you're not alone."

"Brian keeps saying that," Cora said with a half smile. Her shoulders relaxed as his genuine concern trickled over her.

"Well, don't you forget it," Mr. Farris said. "Promise me you won't make any decisions now."

Cora nodded.

"You just let me know if you need anything." Mr. Farris said.

"Thank you. I think since Harold's passed, I've been feeling lost. But I know I have you and Brian." Cora hugged Mr. Farris.

Ruby stepped closer to the two, and Cora detected no feelings from Ruby now. Ruby's ability didn't shield her emotions when she became angry. For the first time, an uneasy feeling made her examine the woman standing next to her while realizing she hadn't investigated Ruby. She'd looked into the McCarthys, Tristan, and Etta.

But she'd assumed Ruby would never kill Harold.

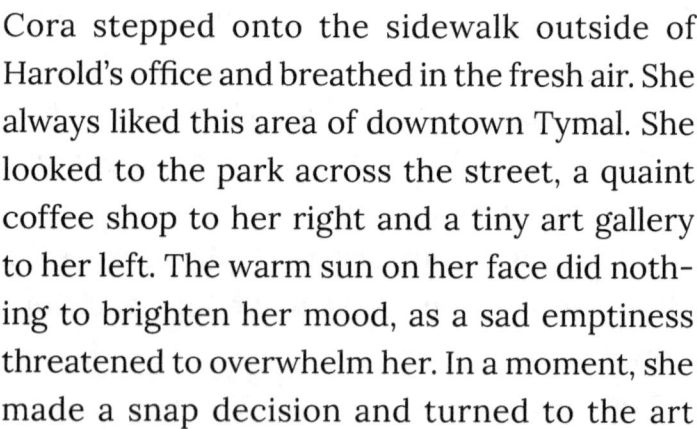

Cora stepped onto the sidewalk outside of Harold's office and breathed in the fresh air. She always liked this area of downtown Tymal. She looked to the park across the street, a quaint coffee shop to her right and a tiny art gallery to her left. The warm sun on her face did nothing to brighten her mood, as a sad emptiness threatened to overwhelm her. In a moment, she made a snap decision and turned to the art gallery. She wanted to run from the turmoil and try to unravel her feelings.

The Alinac was a small neighborhood art gallery supported by the well-to-do parents of their somewhat talented adult offspring. Most of the time, Cora found their art bland, but every so often, one or two pieces surprised her. As she stepped closer, the door slid open, and cool, dry air wafted over her, bringing with it a faint smell of paint.

"Good morning, Ms. Brimble," the Alinac's AI greeted her. She stood in the lobby featuring four painting collections, one photo exhibit, and two laser illustrations. The paintings stood in groups of three and on stands, each highlighted by a spotlight. A photo exhibit depicted the lunar landscape and took up most of the lobby. The laser illustrations showed abstract art that resembled colorful distortions of people and animals. "It's been eight months since you've visited, and we've added several new collections. Follow the floor arrows to reach the first new selection titled 'Lunar Sunrise.'"

"I really want to see the flowers." Cora gazed at the flower collection that could've come straight out of a meadow. The floor arrows changed and directed Cora to a different part of the Alinac. Cora wandered past another exhibit created with dark, dripping paint. She couldn't figure out what the painting depicted and moved on. As she made her way to the flower exhibit, she heard quiet voices murmuring near her. At the very back of the art gallery, Cora found the flowers. She always found flowers calming. She used to hide in the garden behind her family's home when Sophia was particularly cruel. Cora examined each of the flower images with their riotous color and cheery blue skies.

Why couldn't life be like this all the time? she thought.

"Cora, I thought I'd find you here," Brian said with a grin.

Cora turned to face Brian and frowned.

Both of Brian's hand shot up.

"I know. I know. You want to be alone." He came to a stop beside her. "I also think this isn't the time for you to be alone."

"I just wanted some time to work through my feelings. How did you find me?" Cora said in a quiet voice as she turned to a new flower painting.

"Just after you left the office, Dad called me and asked me to check on you." Brian examined

Cora's profile. "I took a guess that you'd come here instead of the park."

"Am I that predictable?" Cora chuckled.

Brian grinned and faced the painting. They both examined it in silence. "You know, I just realized I know this artist."

"Ivy Santos. I met her at the Spencers' tea party a while ago." Cora leaned forward. "She mentioned her exhibit, but I didn't expect too much." Cora tilted her head for a moment. "I like it."

"It's a little too... nice." Brian wrinkled his nose.

"I suppose you like that dark monstrosity near the entrance." Cora pointed, referring to the dark, dripping painting. She turned to Brian with a lopsided smile.

"No. Definitely not." Brian turned to Cora. "Talk to me. What's going on?"

Cora sighed and moved to the next painting.

"I suppose your dad told you I want to sell my mines."

"Yes, but you won't do that." He spoke as if it was a statement rather than a question.

"You know the Farris family is a bit pushy," she said with a small smile.

"Cora, you're the strongest person I know," he said in a quiet voice. "You decide you're going to do something, and you do it." He glanced at her, waiting for her to say something. "Please, don't give up."

She felt her cheeks grow warm..

"I won't do anything right now except find out who murdered Harold. I'm not giving up." She glanced at him. "I've been thinking about the evening I went to visit the McCarthys on my own. I think I went alone because it feels as if I don't have a family anymore. No one to rely on. I suppose I could talk to Aunt Ferna, but she gets upset too easily—I can't tell her everything."

"You know that's not true. You can rely on me, and even my dad." He turned to face her while holding one hand.

"Yeah, I realized that when I spoke to him earlier. I just wanted to say thank you." She glanced at him, and then moved to a new painting.

Brian followed.

"I like this one in blue with the moody sky," he said. "It evokes a restless feeling. It's as if I've so much to do and not enough time to do it."

"Really?" Cora leaned toward the painting. "For me, the feeling is agitation—as if everything is all mixed together and I can't sort it out."

"Interesting how one painting can elicit two different feelings." Brian peered at the painting.

"Hmm..." Cora eyed the painting, admiring the details in the sky.

"I have a theory," he said, turning Cora to face him. "What if Steven is the real murderer?"

Her brows furrowed.

"What'd be his motive?"

"Credits, of course." He dropped his hands to his side. "He's blackmailing people."

"Maybe." She scratched her head, thinking. "I'd think we'd have heard something about that by now."

"Steven's the only person connected to almost everyone at that table when Sophia and Uncle Harold died." He frowned as he leaned toward another painting, which depicted a riot of colors. "Think about it. Messages with no origin, tracking, or sender information. He's the only one who could program nanobots like that."

"I have been thinking. I always get stuck trying to figure out a motive. There're Etta's encrypted vidchats and comms between Sophia and Wesley. All of those communications have no tracking information," she said.

"That must be easy for someone with Steven's skills," he said.

"Actually, it's more difficult than you might think." She stepped to the next painting, depicting cascading shades of pink in a small garden. She paused and examined the painting for a moment. "Anyway, the Net has several layers of checks to verify all tracking information. If the information isn't consistent or the message contains a virus, the system automatically flags the message. Of course, this doesn't stop the spy operations or the military because they've got advanced code the Net can't detect."

"Which means it has to be Steven," he said in a triumphant voice. "He's the only one with military experience."

"I don't know." She knitted her brows in thought. "Remember, he said the person he works for has even more advanced skills."

"That's if you believe him," he scoffed.

"Blackmail isn't Steven's style. He's more likely to take barely legal coding jobs." She continued to the next painting. "Too much green."

"I think it's pretty." He studied the green painting. "The only problem is he doesn't have a motive—that we know of. We should do some digging."

"I have..." She sighed. "He has no footprint on the Net. Even the EGS can't track him."

"I have a few contacts. I'll ask around." Brian smiled. "I think we just need a little proof and the EGS will focus on Steven instead of you."

Cora nodded. "I hope it's that easy."

CHAPTER 21

The next morning, Cora's impatient nail-tapping marked time as she sat on a floral patterned sofa in a small sunroom at the back of her home, facing the garden. She kept her aunt company while waiting for Brian to appear. This was Aunt Ferna's favorite room because it contained a wall of floor-to-ceiling glass windows that surrounded a double door facing the garden. The comfortable room contained a plush sofa and cushioned chairs arranged around a coffee table. Tall potted plants framed one wall and artwork featuring seven types of roses dominated another wall.

"What have you planned for today, dear?" Aunt Ferna took a sip of tea.

Cora stopped tapping her nails.

"I'm going to talk to Brian about a mutual friend." Cora sensed her aunt's radiated tension, which made her mindful not to say too much to upset her.

"Dear, are you looking into Harold's death?" Aunt Ferna placed her cup on the coffee table. "You're already on the EGS's radar, let them handle it."

"We're simply gathering information to give to them." Cora gazed at the blooming azaleas. She wondered how her aunt discovered her investigation when she'd never mentioned it. She didn't want to upset her aunt, but she also had to clear her name. "What're your plans today?" she asked, trying to change the subject.

"Mabel and I are going to a new restaurant downtown." Aunt Ferna grinned. "It's supposed to be authentic Venusian food."

"What does that even mean?" Cora raised an eyebrow. "If humans created the food, it's not really Venusian."

"Shows what you know." A smug expression settled on Aunt Ferna's face. "It's stylish to eat food that's grown in soil from other planets. It adds a unique flavor that only the most sophisticated palates can taste."

Cora breathed a sigh of relief that she'd managed to change the conversation. "Sophisticated palate? Are you sure you aren't fooling your-selves?"

"Oh no. It turns out I can taste the difference," Aunt Ferna said with a hint of pride. "Mabel and I ate at the Lunar Cube a few weeks ago and we could both taste the subtle lunar flavors infused into the food."

"You and I ate at the Martian Moon Cafe and I couldn't taste anything Martian." Cora raised an eyebrow. "Did you taste anything?"

"Of course I did. Simply didn't mention it to you," Aunt Ferna said shifting in her seat.

"I don't know... It sounds like a scam," Cora said. "Did you have to pay any extra credits?"

"Of course not. We just paid for our meals like we would at any restaurant." Aunt Ferna shifted in her seat, not meeting Cora's eyes.

"What aren't you telling me?" Cora asked.

"Nothing... I need to get a little shopping done before I meet Mabel." Aunt Ferna stood. "I'll see you later this afternoon." She brushed past Bri-an. "Good morning dear, can't stop."

Brian jumped out of the way and turned to Cora. "What was that about?"

"I don't know... She and Mabel are up to some-thing, but I think it's harmless," Cora turned to Brian. "Come in, come in."

"How're you feeling today?" Brian sat and poured a cup of tea.

"Better. I think I needed a good night's sleep." Cora leaned forward. "I reviewed our investigation so far. We've never questioned Ruby."

"Ruby! No. She was loyal to Uncle Harold." Brian shook his head and settled on a cushioned seat opposite Cora.

"I know she cared for him, but she may have intentionally or accidentally helped the killer," Cora said.

"I can understand causing his unintentional death, but deliberately doesn't make sense." Brian shook his head. "But it won't hurt to talk to her. Maybe there's something about Sophia and Uncle's deaths we're missing."

"I'm glad you feel that way." Cora grinned. "She's on her way here now."

"You think you have this all figured out?" Brian smirked and took a sip of tea.

"No. I'm just happy we have a new direction to keep digging," Cora said.

"Ms. Ruby Gibson is at the front door," Haley, the home's AI, said.

"Haley, where's Aunt Ferna?" Cora stood.

"Ms. Ferna Robertson has left the house," Haley replied.

Cora grinned and turned to Brian. "Show time." She took a few steps toward the door. "Haley, please show Ruby to the sunroom."

"Ms. Ruby is on her way," Haley said. A few seconds later, Ruby entered.

"Ruby, I'm happy you could make it here on such short notice." Cora gestured toward one of the plush chairs.

"Well, you said it was important." Ruby arranged herself on a seat. "Do you want funeral information? I've made the arrangements. It'll be in a few days."

"I know, and I don't want to take you away from your work, but..." Cora paused and studied Ruby, marveling at how she didn't broadcast her emotions. "It's about Harold and Sophia's deaths. Would you mind answering a few questions for us? We're trying to understand what happened."

"I think you should leave this to the EGS. It's not safe," Ruby said with an edge in her voice. "Remember when we both tried to talk Harold into going to the EGS because Etta said someone murdered Sophia?"

"Yes. I wish he'd listened to you. He might still be alive." Cora spoke in a quiet voice. "But I really can't wait for the EGS. They've decided I'm guilty, and they're not looking anywhere else."

"I see... Very well, I'll try to help you." Ruby settled into her seat. "What would you like to know?"

"Who came up with the idea to host a second dinner party at the Carnation?" Cora asked while surveying Ruby, whose shoulders tensed.

"I don't want to talk about the day Harold passed," Ruby said.

"That's fine. I have questions about the first dinner party when Sophia passed away." Cora said. "Whose idea was it to celebrate Sophia's birthday at the Carnation?"

"Sophia's. It was very popular last year." Ruby gazed through the windows at the garden.

"Did you make the reservations and send the invitation?"

She noticed Ruby's stiff shoulders.

"I made the reservation; Sophia decided who was coming. Only she didn't make a list. Instead, she called me every few days to add people and occasionally remove some." Ruby crossed her arms. "At one point the Carnation couldn't find a table for everyone, and then Sophia changed the list again. It was a miracle we even got a table."

"Did Sophia frequently change her mind like that?" Cora asked.

"Well, you should know, growing up with her," Ruby stood. "Look, I don't know what this is about, but I have work to do."

Cora remained seated and even settled back on the sofa. "You're right. I spent my first five years with Sophia, but then my parents sent me to a boarding school. I only came home for holidays and not all of those. When I was home, Sophia was often outright cruel towards me. There's a lot about Sophia that I don't know. Please, help me understand."

Ruby hesitated before she regained her chair.

"After Sophia settled on the list," she continued. "The menu changed several times. In the end, everyone ordered from the Carnation's standard menu. The thing that really irked me was I'm... I was Harold's personal assistant, not hers. She should've hired her own secretary. She certainly needed one." Ruby shifted in her seat. "When they first got married, she kept insisting I arrange dinner parties for her. I tried talking to Harold, but it didn't do any good. She expected everyone to drop what they were doing and do whatever she wanted, and Harold was happy to go along with it."

Cora noticed Ruby's tone never wavered, and she never broadcast any emotions. The woman sitting across from her still wore a composed expression.

She needed a different way to make Ruby emotional.

"I remember the night Sophia died," Cora said. "I arrived with Sophia and Harold, but you were already there. You hugged Sophia, and I remember thinking how unusual that was. You're normally reserved." Cora braced herself in case Ruby radiated her emotions. She didn't want to shield herself, but she also didn't want to be overwhelmed. She launched into her next question. "Why did you hug Sophia?"

Ruby chuckled. "I don't remember. That was nearly a year ago." She leaned forward. "Wait, I remember now. I also hugged Harold and you. I must've simply been in a good mood."

Even though Ruby laughed, Cora felt a faint spike of unease from her.

"Who arranged the events of the evening?" Cora asked. "At the party, Sophia boasted that *her* plans included dancing, a toast, dinner, and a cake."

"I arranged the events, but Sophia decided when they'd happen," Ruby said with a neutral expression.

"So you did the work, but Sophia took the credit. Did she do that with other events?" Cora asked.

"Yes." Ruby frowned. "She frequently took advantage of my time, even after Harold had a talk with her."

This time, Cora definitely felt it. A small spark of... Hatred? Cora braced herself for her next set of questions.

"Look, could we delay this... interrogation until after the funeral?" Ruby stood.

Cora opened her mouth to reply, but Brian interrupted her.

"I think that'd be okay."

Brian stood and grasped Ruby's hand.

Cora shot to her feet.

"Why did you kill Harold?" she said, her heartbeat leaping in her chest. "I know you loved him. Why did you do it?"

Cora's eyes bored into Ruby's.

Ruby's mouth opened and closed several times, but nothing came out.

"I see why you killed Sophia," Cora continued. "You hated her, and you loved Harold." She took a few steps toward Ruby and spoke in a softer voice. "You're an Askovian, but you worked for Harold. Did you stay to be close to him? Please tell me—I just want to understand."

Ruby shook and tears rolled down her cheeks.

"I'm not a disgusting Askovian like you," she spat the words out with a shudder. "I have a neurowall implant."

It doesn't work perfectly—I've felt your anger several times when you got angry, she thought.

"That must've been expensive," Cora said instead.

"It was worth every penny," Ruby said with an edge to her voice. Her tears dried on her cheeks, but she continued to tremble. "Askovians are a cancer—they take and take until the rest of us die."

"Ruby, please have a seat." Brian spoke in a low, gentle voice as he stepped to her side.

Surrounded by Brian and Cora, Ruby turned between the two with frantic head movements.

"Shut up! Stop talking!" She yelled. "This is all your fault!" Ruby screamed as her eyes bored into Cora.

Cora received the full force of Ruby's beamed hatred as it overwhelmed her neurowall.

"You were supposed to die! It should've been you. Not my Harold!" Ruby lunged at Cora, who scampered back several paces. Brian caught Ruby's arms and held her while she broke into loud, wracking sobs. Cora shielded herself from Ruby's despair, which threatened to drown and swallow her whole. As gently as he could without allowing her to lunge toward Cora again, Brian guided Ruby back to her chair, where she continued to wail. After several minutes, her weeping quieted to a whimper.

"My Feeler abilities are completely different from Sophia's," Cora said in a quiet voice. "I can't force people to do things. I only sense their emotions."

"Just because you're not as manipulative as Sophia doesn't mean you aren't vile," Ruby's voice dripped venom.

"How am I awful?" Cora focused on Ruby, trying to understand.

"You killed Harold." Ruby wiped her face as more tears streamed over her cheeks.

"How did I kill Harold?" Cora asked in a soft voice. "Is this about the nanobots? My guess is you hired Steven to program the microscopic robots, but why did Harold die instead of me?"

Ruby stared at her lap, wiping an occasional tear on her face.

"I don't know who Steven is. Something went wrong. I gave him your DNA. Something went wrong."

Cora decided to try another tack. "Brian, please call the EGS."

"No! Don't call them!" Ruby jumped out of her seat, causing Brian to take one of her arms. "You don't understand. We'll all be in danger if you do that!"

"How will we be in danger?" Cora studied Ruby's face.

Ruby opened and closed her mouth several times as if to say something. But she remained silent.

"Brian, do you remember Steven doing this?" Cora's lips drew to a thin line.

"Yes. It looked as if he wanted to talk, but couldn't," Brian said, examining Ruby.

"Ruby, how did I kill Harold?"

Ruby glanced from Cora to Brian and still said nothing.

Cora scratched her head, thinking. "Please, tell me."

"Nanobots!" Ruby gasped, as if surprised she could speak. A frisson of fear raced over her face, and she tried to wiggle her arm out of Brian's grasp. "Let me go!"

Cora lowered her shield in tiny steps. She wanted to understand Ruby, who broadcast a tangled mix of anxiety, misery, hatred, and gloom. But it didn't overwhelm Cora anymore.

"Who programmed the nanobots?" Cora's raised voice got Ruby's attention, and she stopped struggling against Brian's grasp.

"I don't know, alright!" Ruby yelled.

Cora maintained a level voice. "How did you launch the nanobots?"

Ruby wiped her eyes. "It was the simplest thing in the world. I hugged Sophia." Her face changed to a half smile while she glanced from Cora to Brian. "The nanobots traveled from my skin to Sophia's." She chuckled. "Don't you see how funny that is? I hugged the woman who stole my Harold and at the same time killed her." She guffawed.

"Ruby, I'm confused." Cora surveyed Ruby, who continued to broadcast a jumbled mix of anger, sadness, fear, and despair. "You also hugged me before dinner, but I didn't die. Why?"

"You're so stupid!" Ruby smirked. "They were programmed for Sophia's DNA, not yours." Her smile fell. "The nanobots killed Sophia, and then

I should've had Harold." Her shoulders sagged. Brian coaxed her back to her chair, where she crumpled. He mouthed EGS to Cora, who nodded while he left the room. A moment later, Ruby covered her face and wept.

Cora shielded herself again, afraid of being overwhelmed by Ruby's sadness.

Fifteen minutes later, Agent Lewis arrived dressed in his usual brown jumpsuit. He took a seat on the sofa next to Cora, who repressed a shudder to hide her dislike. He activated a recording mode on his bracelet and asked for everyone's permission to record them.

Cora explained what they'd discovered from Ruby. She also pointed out that a type of mental block prevented Ruby from discussing the circumstances of Harold's death, but she could explain Sophia's.

"Is that what Feelers call 'scrambling your emotions?'" Agent Lewis asked.

"Yes. Truly advanced Feelers like Sophia can make you feel things that aren't real, and attach those feelings to unrelated memories, creating a tangled nest of emotions," Cora said. "It becomes impossible to talk about these events with any clarity, if at all. Someone has done this to Ruby and Steven. Even if you caught Steven, you wouldn't be able to get any information from him."

Ruby explained how she administered microscopic robots to Sophia. Someone had programmed the nanobots to seek Sophia's DNA, kill her at a specific time, and then self-destruct. Ruby never spoke to the programmer.

"Thank you, Ms. Gibson." Agent Lewis gazed at Ruby. "Is there anything else you can say concerning Sophia's murder?"

"No," Ruby spoke in a quiet voice and stared at her lap.

"One more thing, Harold died by accident," Cora said. "I was the real target. It turns out the block on Ruby's mind doesn't stop her from speaking her opinions."

Agent Lewis turned to Cora. "It seems you may have nothing to do with your sister's murder. We'll continue the investigation into Mr. Albright's death."

"I have something else to add." Cora glanced at Brian for strength. "A couple of nights ago, Brian and I ran into Steven."

"Why didn't you contact us immediately?" Agent Lewis's eyes bored into Cora.

"Because as soon as we finished our conversation, he disappeared," Cora said sharply. She tried not to let him make her angry, but resentment bubbled in her stomach. "You won't be able to find him. He's off the Net."

Agent Lewis eyed her for a moment. "Alright. What did Steven Marsh have to say?"

Cora waited a moment to allow herself to calm down. "Steven admitted to cloaking Sophia and Wesley's affair, feeding information to EGS to get me arrested, but he didn't program the nanobots."

"I see, but we suspected as much already," Agent Lewis said.

"The same day we saw Steven," Cora said. "Brian and I visited Etta. There is a contradiction between what Etta and Ruby said. Using Etta's information, I killed Sophia and Harold to inherit their mines. If you believe Ruby, Sophia and I were supposed to die, but the cause of death should have been hidden due to the dissolving nanobots."

"You two have been busy," Agent Lewis glanced at Brian and Cora. "Okay, we'll follow up with Ms. Johanson." He stood and ambled to

Ruby. "Ms. Gibson, you're under arrest for the murder of Sophia Albright."

He read Ruby her rights and, several minutes later, left with her.

"This isn't over. Someone told Steven and Ruby what to do." Cora paced to the wall of windows. "What scares me is that someone with very advanced Askovian abilities appears to be behind this."

"I know what you mean." Brian joined her at the windows. "I've never heard of an ability that stops others from talking."

"Something else is bothering me." Cora gazed at the hummingbirds darting from flower to flower.

"You mean why we've never heard of this new ability?" Brian asked.

"That, and something else." Cora turned to Brian. "Someone killed Sophia and, as a result, her assets passed to me, not her husband. Is it possible the killer expected Harold to inherit, and that's why they killed him?"

"The timing doesn't make sense." His eyebrows knitted together. "You inherited her mine months ago."

"Right. So, if we believe Ruby, I was supposed to die, then the Brimble mine would've passed to Aunt Ferna." She frowned. "I think I know who's behind this whole mess."

He smirked. "I hope you're not suggesting that sweet old lady tried to kill you."

"No, no! We have to call the EGS," she said in a raised voice. "Brian, send a message to the EGS, and I'll see if Agent Lewis is still out front."

"What're you talking about?" Brian said. "What's going on?"

Cora jogged toward the sunroom's entrance when a tall, attractive man with the same green eyes as Sophia stepped into the room. "Oliver!"

Chapter 22

"Good morning, Cousin." Oliver strolled into the sunroom and came to a stop facing Cora. "You always were a smart thing. Sometimes a little too smart."

Cora gaped at Oliver, stunned to see him in her home.

In her shock, she didn't have time to shield her mind, and she sensed Oliver's invading presence. This is how it felt when Sophia made her feel things that weren't real. For several moments, she couldn't think or run or do anything.

"What're you doing here? Get o—" Brian said in a raised voice, but suddenly stopped talking.

Cora tried to turn her head and check on Brian, but her neck wouldn't turn. Instead, waves of terror washed over her as she tried to turn and run. Her legs wouldn't move. Cora's stomach rolled over, and she wondered if she could even vomit.

Will I choke and die? she thought.

Oliver stepped around her and out of her sight. A moment later, Ruby scurried into the room holding a large kitchen knife. Her impassive face studied Cora, while she raised the knife with a slow, deliberate motion, ready to strike.

What are you doing here? she thought. *Where's Agent Lewis?*

Ruby stepped out of view.

Cora tried to make her eyes follow Ruby, but fresh waves of panic threatened to swallow her.

"Cora, are you okay?" Haley, the home's AI, asked. "I'm detecting elevated stress hormones."

"Haley, deactivate. Code twelve-thirty-seven," Oliver said.

"Cora, turn around," Oliver said in a commanding voice she'd never heard before from him.

Cora's legs and feet obeyed, and less than a second later she faced Oliver seated on the sofa. In her peripheral vision, she saw Brian sitting in a cushioned chair opposite Oliver. Brian's placid face showed no emotion, and Cora realized Oliver controlled him, too.

"I suppose you're wondering what's going on?" Oliver said with an oily smile. "You know, Cousin, I've always admired you. No, really. You're the sort of person my mom wished I could be. But I'd rather kill myself than live such a dull life." Oliver chuckled.

Ideas tumbled through Cora's mind as she tried to think of a way to remove Oliver's control. Moving increased the anxiety, but she could wrack her mind trying to come up with a plan.

"You want to know what I've planned? You've such a quest for knowledge," Oliver grinned. "Ruby's going to hand you a knife, and you're going to kill Brian. You'll confess to the killing and go to a prison colony." Oliver stood and stepped closer to Cora. "You can't inherit if you're in prison. Don't worry, you won't remember this part of this conversation."

Somehow, the thought of killing Brian raised Cora above the ocean of anxiety. She remembered what it was like to fight Sophia. *This isn't real*, she thought over and over until her own emotions flowed back to her. The ocean of fear receded to a raging river, and she stood on dry land. Her own fears helped create the raging river, but she ignored the turbulent waterway. Instead, she focused on dry land and tranquil emotions.

"Nice try." Oliver frowned. "You can't escape me. I've controlled Steven, Ruby, and sometimes even Sophia."

"Sit down," Oliver commanded.

Cora moved to a chair opposite the sofa and slowly lowered onto the seat. She sensed Oliver's invading mind as tiny licks of fear lapped at her feet. Now seated, she couldn't move again. When she tried to make the smallest movements, the fear lapped over her feet and up her calves. When she remained still, it retreated to her feet.

Oliver straightened and moved to her side. "Maybe the plan would work better if Brian killed you." He glanced at Brian, who got up from his chair, stood on shaky feet, then stumble-walked towards Cora. She saw the blind terror in his eyes as he raised an empty hand, ready to strike.

Cora forced herself to ignore Brian. He stood in her peripheral vision, which made it difficult to see him, and she needed to maintain a calm, controlled mind. Instead, she surveyed Ruby's detached and composed expression. She wondered if Oliver had control over her, too.

"What do you think?" Oliver smirked. "Which one should kill?"

Ruby peered at Cora.

"She's like her sister—she'll fight you at every step." She turned to Brian. "He's weaker and easier to control. Have him kill her with the knife. You'll still get two mines."

"Yes," Oliver stood. "What you're saying makes sense, but I've always loved a challenge. I controlled Steven, who also fought very well."

"And now he's disappeared. He could still go to the EGS." Ruby stood and paced toward Brian. "If she escapes your control, things won't go well for either of us. But you can make him say and do anything."

"It won't matter if Steven goes to the EGS," Oliver said in a condescending voice. "I've scrambled his emotions enough. He won't be able to recall any programming he did for me."

"Is... Is that what you did to me?" Ruby asked in a quiet voice.

"Only for your own safety," Oliver said in a sickly, sweet voice. "If the EGS tries to question you, you can't incriminate yourself."

"I also can't tell them what you've done," Ruby said with an edge to her voice.

Oliver ignored Ruby and turned from Brian to Cora. "I've decided to play with my cousin instead. By the time they find her, they'll think she's insane."

Brian lowered his arm and shuffled to his seat. After he sat, a single tear rolled down his cheek.

Cora decided not to use any part of her body to fight because he used her own emotions to control her. When she tried to move a toe or finger, her mind created debilitating fear. She needed her shield but trying to erect the shield would also alert Oliver. What could she do that her cousin wouldn't notice?

"Cousin, I feel you thinking," Oliver said in a sing-song voice. "You can't outwit me, but you can try."

Cora ignored Oliver and focused on Ruby. She hoped Oliver didn't have control over her. She thought her new idea may not work anyway because of Ruby's neurowall shielding her emotions.

Cora examined the empty sofa opposite while allowing herself to feel any emotions Ruby may be transmitting. At first, she detected nothing from Ruby.

"What's she doing, Oliver?" Ruby asked. "I don't like this. We need to get out of here before Ferna returns."

"My mom won't be back for hours." Oliver chuckled. "I think you're right. She's doing something, but I don't know what yet."

Cora sensed a faint spasm of fear from Ruby. When Ruby became very upset, she transmitted her emotions loud and clear. A spark of an idea crossed Cora's mind.

"What about that EGS agent?" Ruby asked. "Don't you think the EGS will come to investigate what's happened to him?"

"We'll be gone before then," Oliver chuckled. "Anyway, I scrambled his emotions. It'll take weeks before they understand him. They'll assume cousin Cora attacked him, of course."

A fresh burst of Ruby's fear radiated throughout the room. Oliver guffawed and turned to Ruby. "Don't worry, my pet. I won't scramble you."

So Ruby did what Oliver said, but she also feared him. Cora pondered how she could use that to her advantage.

"Now, what should we do first?" Oliver eyed Cora like a cat playing with a mouse.

Cora detected Oliver's mind withdrawing one tiny step and wondered if she'd be able to erect her shield before he attacked her again.

"There you go, little Cousin." Oliver sat on the sofa opposite Cora. "Speak."

Cora cleared her throat and waited for a panic or terror attack. She relaxed her shoulders when she realized Oliver had released some of his control.

"Why're you doing this?"

A shout of laughter escaped Oliver.

"Is that the best you can do?" He leaned forward on his elbows. "I want your mines, you idiot. Once you're out of the way, Mom inherits, and she can never say no to me."

He grinned.

"Why not arrange a steady income from the mines? You could've talked Sophia or even Harold into it." Cora worked to think of questions to keep him talking. Eventually, someone would come to the house.

"That question is a little better." Oliver settled onto the sofa. "I used to receive an income from the Brimble mine. Then, I overspent a few times, asked for an advance every so often, needed funds to cover gambling debts… You get the picture. Harold cut me off."

"I see. Your lifestyle already matched your share of the mine's income. You couldn't go back to living without it." Cora continued to wrack her brain for an idea.

Oliver smirked. "Stupid Harold had no idea what I could do—what I'm capable of."

"So, you killed Sophia with nanobots programmed by Steven, but Ruby administered them with a hug," Cora spoke and did her level best not to move too much and trigger a panic attack.

"Well, at least you're not stupid like your sister," Oliver said. "I think I'm going to enjoy playing with you."

"You hired Steven to hide Sophia and Wesley's affair. Was that to divert suspicion from the McCarthys?" Cora surveyed Oliver.

"Another good one. The answer is yes." Oliver chuckled. "Made it easier to incriminate you."

"I suppose Etta was just a distraction for the EGS and me," Cora said.

"That part of my plan didn't exactly work out. Her prediction would've thrown suspicion on you," Oliver said. "Didn't matter. We ended up here with you under my control."

"What confuses me is, how did you get Ruby to kill Harold?" Cora turned her head to face

Ruby and was relieved that the ocean of terror didn't return. At the same time, her new idea solidified into a plan.

"That was an accident." Oliver glanced at Ruby. "I molded Steven's emotions, which influenced him to create the nanobots. He fought me, of course—he didn't like killing. So I scrambled his emotions after he programmed the nanobots." Oliver chortled. "He also underestimated me. He became so confused he thought I programmed the nanobots."

Cora received the spears of venom mixed with pain launched by Ruby. Oliver must've sensed them, too.

"It's hard to believe that was a fluke," Cora said in a thoughtful tone. "With Sophia and Harold dead, you'll have access to two mines once you get me out of the way. Right now, the Martian mine is worth four times the Brimble mine on Ganymede. Are you telling me it's just by chance that you received that amount of wealth? What exactly did you tell Steven to program?"

Ruby turned and eyed Oliver.

"Tell me she's lying," she said. "Tell me you didn't kill Harold for a mine."

"I don't have to justify myself to you," Oliver said, his voice turning cold. "You do as I tell you and don't ask questions."

Cora perceived Ruby's rumbling emotions. It was like watching a smoldering volcano with steam leaking from the cracks and the ground shaking just before the big blowout. She just had to push Ruby a little further.

"So, I'm just curious. Have you been helping Oliver since the beginning?" Cora furrowed her eyebrows. "You know when I dropped you off at the hotel and we met Oliver, did he ever get on the shuttle for Lunar City?"

"Oliver's been on Earth for months," Ruby said with a note of disgust. "I've been helping him the whole time."

"So, I guess my real question is, what's your cut of the income from the two mines?" Cora asked.

Ruby glared at Oliver, crossed her arms, and paced to the wall of windows. She stared into the garden, but Cora sensed the volcano move one step closer to the explosion.

"So, you get nothing, and your beloved Harold is dead. Doesn't seem fair, does it?" Cora concentrated on maintaining a calm, undisturbed mind.

"All I wanted was Harold," Ruby spoke with an edge. "Now he's gone."

"Shut up!" Oliver sprang to his feet, glaring at Cora. "I see what you're doing—you won't turn her against me. I'm in control."

"You know what I miss most about Harold?" Cora asked in a wistful voice, ignoring Oliver. "His kindness. It made him a skilled teacher and an even better listener. And now we're never going to see him again."

"Nooooo!" Ruby yelled and ran toward Oliver with the knife held high, ready to sink it into him.

Oliver whipped around to face Ruby and narrowed his eyes. Ruby stumbled and flopped to the ground, unconscious, the knife clattering to the floor beside her.

In that moment, Cora erected her shield, pushing all of Oliver's mind out. Oliver turned back to Cora, narrowing his eyes, but it was too late. She'd regained control of her mind.

She had little time before Oliver would attack her shield. Her chest tightened with fear, wondering if Oliver still had control of Brian.

She used her Feeler abilities to probe Brian's mind and shield him from Oliver, who in his shock and rage, no longer had a hold on Brian's mind. It'd been years since she'd shielded another person, but she breathed a sigh of relief when it worked.

Oliver's strong energy pummeled her shield, and Cora cried out. It was nothing like she'd experienced before, and it took all of her strength to maintain her shield while protecting Brian. Sharp spasms of pain leaped through her brain, and she folded her arms over her head, trying to stop the charge.

Suddenly, Oliver's strength increased, and Cora rushed to find the energy to hold on to her shield. In a flash, she realized his increased power resulted from not controlling Ruby any longer. She decreased her shield protecting Brian's brain and sent energy pulses to Ruby.

Almost immediately, Ruby began blinking, as if waking after sleep. Ruby raised her head in small increments and surveyed the room. As she took everything in, her face twisted in hatred, but for once she didn't look at Cora. Instead, her eyes bored into Oliver's back. Ruby searched the floor and found the knife.

Pulling herself to her feet, she raised her arm as if ready to strike.

No! Not yet! Cora thought. *Move closer first.*

Horror marred Cora's face when she saw Ruby move. She stumble-walked as if part of her wanted to run and the other wanted to tip-toe. Her arm hung in the air at an awkward angle, as if ready to attack but facing the wrong way.

Terror marked Ruby's eyes.

Cora now controlled Ruby and had even given her a command.

"No, I'm not her," Cora said in a timid voice while withdrawing her energy from Ruby's mind. Cora always prided herself on not being anything like her sister, who loved to control and manipulate people. She'd behaved just like Sophia and the shame gripped her chest.

Ruby stopped and shook her head. She blinked again.

"What're you doing?" Oliver glanced at Ruby.

Ruby's eyebrows rose with alarm as she refocused on Cora. "What are you?" She glanced at Oliver. "She's one of you."

"What're you talking about?" Oliver, distracted, paused his offensive against Cora's mind and turned to face Ruby.

"You're all monsters." Ruby took one step away from Cora and Oliver. "Why didn't I see it earlier? You control and manipulate everyone around you."

"You, Cousin?" Oliver snickered. "I didn't know you had it in you." He walked to Cora's chair, placing his hands on her armrests and edging his face close to hers. "I've always thought of you as a child."

Thinking of goading Ruby again, Cora focused on her anguished face as she paced behind Oliver. "Don't you care that Ruby sacrificed everything for you?" Cora asked.

Oliver guffawed. "What new game are you playing now?"

"There's no game," Cora said in a quiet voice. "Ruby worked for Harold for years. After Sophia died, they could have made a life together. Now Harold's gone, and she has no one left."

Ruby's mouth formed a grim line. After a moment of indecision, she adjusted her grip on the knife. Her eyes bored into Oliver's back, and she charged.

Ruby reached Oliver and her knife sunk into his back. Suddenly, Oliver's attack ceased, and Cora sagged into her chair, panting.

Oliver yelled out in pain, rage, and fear. He turned to face Ruby, whose eyes rolled back into her head as she fell to the floor. Oliver fell to his knees. "Medic. Send the medic."

Haley didn't respond.

Cora pushed herself to her feet and on trembling legs, picked her way around Oliver to check on Brian. Relief flooded through her as Brian blinked and gazed around the room, confused. She pushed a button on her bracelet and sent an emergency distress call to the EGS.

"This is Earth Global Security. What is the nature of your emergency?" a robotic operator asked.

"Medical emergency. Oliver Robertson has been stabbed. He's losing a lot of blood." Cora glanced at Oliver, who now lay on the floor whimpering in pain. She made her way toward a blank wall, looking for the medipad.

"Haley, activate." Cora turned to Oliver. "How did you deactivate Haley?"

Oliver didn't respond as he'd passed out.

"He's losing too much blood." Brian raced to Oliver and put pressure on the knife wound. "Where's the medipad?"

"It's here." Cora examined a blank wall, trying to figure out how to extract the medipad. "It easily pops out when Haley's running. I don't remember how to get it out manually." Cora pressed several spots as she darted along the wall.

CHAPTER 23

Two EGS medics dressed in red and white jumpsuits entered the sunroom. "We received a distress call..."

"Here," Brian called. "He has a knife wound."

As the EGS medics worked on Oliver, Agent Lewis and nine more EGS agents rushed into the sunroom. He took a moment to examine the scene and deployed the other agents throughout the room. He loped to Ruby's body.

"She's alive, but I think he's scrambled her emotions." He examined the skin just above her ear and pressed. A moment later, a shiny metal spider-like robot exited the dent in her scalp. Agent Lewis removed the robot and handed it to another EGS agent. Next, he pulled a shiny metal button from his pocket and pressed it into the space just over her ear. After a few seconds, it burrowed into her head. He pressed a button on his bracelet, which created a floating screen over Ruby. On the screen, he selected a few buttons, and something whirred to life.

"How's he doing?" Agent Lewis called to the medics and took a couple of steps toward Oliver. They murmured, but Cora couldn't hear what they said. Agent Lewis placed a shiny button just over Oliver's ear. A floating screen appeared over Oliver's body and Agent Lewis selected a different set of buttons compared to Ruby's.

"What did you do to them?" Cora took tentative steps toward the medics.

"I've upgraded Ruby's neurowall to military-grade—it'll rebalance her emotions faster than her old one. Oliver also has a new military-grade neurowall which will completely repress his Feeler abilities."

Agent Lewis stood.

"We've been looking for him for months. We got word he was in Tymal, but we couldn't find him," Agent Lewis said with an edge in his voice. "He's wanted in Lunar City for a few deaths."

"You've known about him, and you put so much pressure on me," Cora said in a raised voice.

"We didn't know he resided here until a few months ago and we didn't know of his involvement with Mr. and Ms. Albright's deaths," Agent Lewis said. He pressed a button on his bracelet, creating a floating screen. He selected a few more buttons on the screen. "Let's have a seat."

Cora made her way unsteadily to the sofa and pulled Brian along with her. They settled on the sofa opposite Agent Lewis. For the first time, she studied Agent Lewis and noticed bags under bloodshot eyes, thinning plastered blond hair, and a tense, hunted look. Every so often, he checked the room as if he expected something bad to happen. He didn't broadcast any emotions, but she still thought he seemed fearful.

"I'm not trying to be rude, but you don't look good," Cora said.

"You don't know Oliver Robertson like I do," Agent Lewis settled into the chair. "He scrambled the emotions of normal people for profit and fun. It's been his signature for years." Agent Lewis spat out the last sentence. "It took us years to track him down. Every time we cornered him, he'd use his abilities to escape. It took us a few more years to develop the tech to defend ourselves. We finally got him—he'll be wearing that controller for the rest of his life."

"Oh, I didn't know," Cora said, nonplussed.

"When I left earlier with Ms. Gibson, I encountered Oliver Robertson on your front lawn." Agent Lewis scowled. "He must've scrambled my emotions again, even though I have a neurowall implant that should've protected me. I didn't wake until other EGS units arrived. The implant rebalanced my emotions, but it takes a little while to fully recover."

At least I understand why he looks so disturbed, she thought.

"How do you know Oliver's new neurowall will work on him?" Cora asked. "He's incredibly powerful."

"Robertson will stay sedated until we can get him to a safe facility." He selected a few buttons on the floating screen, letting them know the official recording started, and asked them to identify themselves. He turned to Cora. "How long have you known Oliver Robertson resided on Earth?"

"I didn't know he was here," Cora said in a firm voice. "A little over a week ago, Ruby said she escorted him to the shuttle for Lunar City, which I now know was a lie."

"Please explain in as much detail as possible what happened here today," Agent Lewis said in his customary bland voice.

"He arrived with Ruby and tried to kill me." Cora shivered, reliving the frightening emotions. She explained the sequence of events that occurred after Oliver appeared in the sunroom doorway.

"So Oliver had Mr. Albright killed, so that you'd inherit his mine." Agent Lewis said.

"Yes. It's been nearly a year since Sophia died, so I've been wondering what slowed Oliver down." Cora responded with a thoughtful expression. "He mentioned that Steven fought him. A Feeler like Oliver can't really make you do something completely against your nature unless he tricks you. I'd guess, but you'd have to check with Oliver, that when Steven created the first set of nanobots, Oliver scrambled his emotions around the event. But Steven knew he'd done something wrong. When Oliver tried to get Steven to create a new set of killer nanobots, Steven disappeared. Oliver came to Earth to find him, and after several months, tracked him down."

Agent Lewis exhaled and seemed to deflate. "What a complicated case. It's still not wrapped up. We can't find Steven Marsh."

"Thing is, if Steven doesn't want to be found, you won't find him." Cora's eyebrows knit. "If you're willing to wait, he'll resurface again, probably looking for more credits."

"All of this happened while I was under Oliver's control," Brian said, a confused look on his face. "I feel so useless." He sighed. "I didn't help you with anything."

"Yes, you did. You were my reason to keep fighting. I'm just happy you're alive and not scrambled," Cora said with a small smile.

A few hours later, Aunt Ferna raced into the sunroom from her lunch date. Her faced marred with panic, she studied the few remaining EGS agents wrapping up their investigation. Most of the EGS officers left earlier with Oliver and Ruby.

"I saw the EGS vehicles out front. What happened here?"

Cora stood and made her way to her aunt, with Brian in tow. "Aunt Ferna, how was your lunch?"

"Tell me what's going on," Aunt Ferna said with wide, frightened eyes.

Cora exchanged a glance with Brian.

"Let's go outside and talk." She hooked an arm under her aunt's and guided her through the double glass doors into the garden. They walked until they reached Cora's favorite feature. The early afternoon sun reflected in the fountain water, so they retreated to a nearby bench. Under the shade of a tree, she listened to birds chirping and bees buzzing from one flower to the next. She inhaled the faint scents of the garden, relieved to have her life back. As she turned to Aunt Ferna, a heaviness returned while she organized her thoughts to explain everything. Cora and Aunt Ferna settled themselves on the bench, and Brian rested on a low garden wall.

"More than a year ago, Oliver got into a huge fight with Harold when he cut off Oliver's credits. Do you remember?"

"Yes, Harold was horrible to him," Aunt Ferna said.

Cora and Brian exchanged glances.

"In any case, Oliver had a huge amount of debt and needed to pay it back. So he created a plan to take Sophia's mine." Cora paused and studied her aunt's radiated concern.

"Oliver could be a little high-strung, but he'd never really hurt anyone," Aunt Ferna said with watery eyes.

"Before Sophia's murder, Oliver hired a man named Steven Marsh to hide any evidence of Sophia and Wesley's affair from the Net," Cora said, studying her aunt.

"The EGS questioned me about their affair. They thought Sophia might have confided in me." Aunt Ferna said. "But we were never that close. How does Sophia and McCarthy's affair fit in?" Aunt Ferna shifted on the bench.

"He hid it at first so that it wouldn't be a distraction to the EGS's investigation," Cora said. "Steven programmed the nanobots for Oliver who convinced Ruby to help him. She assumed she'd get Harold after Sophia passed, and she agreed to hug Sophia, transferring the nanobots on her skin. In about thirty minutes, they killed her."

Aunt Ferna nodded while a single tear rolled down her cheek.

Cora sensed the rolling waves of her aunt's deep sadness.

"After Sophia passed, the attorneys transferred Sophia's mine to me," Cora said. "Also, Steven fed the EGS information about Sophia and Wesley's relationship. He influenced their investigation by making Vivian and Wesley appear innocent. He made sure the EGS knew Vivian was aware of the fling and that Wesley had broken things off before Sophia passed."

"Oliver's plans should've moved more quickly. I think something happened between Oliver and Steven. Maybe they had a fight because they made no progress for several months."

"Oliver probably had a change of heart. He's not a bad person," Aunt Ferna said.

Cora sensed Aunt Ferna's lessening sadness.

"In any case, things started moving again a few weeks ago. Steven fed the EGS incriminating information about me. Oliver hired that Seer to say someone murdered Sophia. Then Harold died."

"It was that Steven fellow. Oliver had nothing to do with Harold." Aunt Ferna said in a high-pitched voice.

"No," Cora said, receiving her aunt's radiated panic. "Are you sure you want me to continue? The story will only get darker."

"Go ahead," Aunt Ferna said in a quiet voice as her radiated panic decreased.

"At this point in the story, there's some disagreement. Ruby says the plan was to reprogram the nanobots for my DNA and have me die, just like Sophia. From her point of view, Harold died accidentally." She paused and waited for Aunt Ferna, who nodded. "But that's not what happened. Oliver needed Harold to die first so that I would inherit another mine. Then Oliver planned to scramble my emotions or have me end my life."

"After you, I inherit your mines, and I always give Oliver what he wants." Aunt Ferna sighed, but she didn't shed any more tears.

Cora only detected the deep rivers of Aunt Ferna's sadness. "I'm so sorry."

She hugged her aunt.

"His father always warned me not to be too permissive." A bitter laugh escaped Aunt Ferna. "But I never could say no to him."

"Aunt, you're just a very kind and loving person." Cora squeezed her shoulders. "When my mom and dad passed away, you were always there for me."

"It's not your fault Oliver made bad choices," Brian said.

"Thank you, both." Aunt Ferna climbed to her feet. "I need to be alone for a little while." She turned and meandered back to the house.

"Poor Aunt Ferna," Brian said. "She looked so stricken."

Cora sighed. "I know. I wish I could fix things, but she had to know the truth." She remained silent for a moment.

"Something's bothering you," Brian said. "Spill—"

"It's nothing... Do you think I'm a bad person?" Cora examined something on her lap.

Brian chuckled. "What're you talking about? Of course you're not bad."

Cora stood and paced to the fountain. Brian followed a moment later. She struggled to ignore the debate in her head before deciding to get help.

"You always say I'm not alone... Brian, I accidentally took control of Ruby's mind. I tried to help her, but instead gave her a command. When I realized what I'd done, I immediately stopped, but..."

"Now you know you have the same Feeler abilities as Sophia and Oliver." Brian grasped both of her hands. "Do you know the most interesting part about your comparison? You, Sophia, and Oliver had a chance to control others. The other two abused their powers, but you stopped. Even when we were being attacked, you made a better choice. You all had the same options, and you made different choices." He kissed both of her hands. "Of course you're not bad."

A warmth spread over Cora's cheeks, and she started to pull her hands away, but Brian leaned forward and enveloped her in a gentle hug. After a moment, she relaxed into it.

"So, you're not the perfect Brimble you thought you were," Brian chortled.

"I actually thought I was better than Sophia and Oliver because I couldn't manipulate emotions." Cora gazed into the fountain. "I've learned more about my flaws in the past few days than the past thirty years."

Cora turned her head to the sky and watched a tiny bird swoop on to a nest. The smell of flowering plants lifted her spirits. "I really miss Harold. But I'm glad his and Sophia's killer will be brought to justice, and I'm so happy my family has expanded to include the Farris clan. Now, I know I'm not alone."

***

To enjoy more cozy mystery science fiction, pick up *Movers, Mines, and Murder*(https://katherinesbooks.com/movers).

Please Leave an Honest Review

Authors thrive on reviews. These reviews help other readers decide whether to buy the book. To write a review, simply go back to the website where you purchased this book, provide a star rating, and add a couple of sentences explaining why you liked the book. Thank you for your review.

Review Link (https://katherinesbooks.com/feeler_review)

WOULD YOU LIKE ANOTHER SCI-FI WHODUNIT?

Want to know how it all began? Dive into *Short Stories from the Feeler Universe* (https://katherinesbooks.com/sci-fi-short-story/), and once you join my newsletter, read this thrilling short story from *The Feeler* series! This prequel takes you to the very beginning, where Cora uses her unique Feeler abilities to unravel a gripping whodunit.

Books

Standalone Books

The Puzzle Safe Mystery
https://katherinesbooks.com/psmamz
The Runaway Martian
https://katherinesbooks.com/runawaymartia
namz
***

The Feeler Series Books

The Feeler (Book 1)
katherinesbooks.com/feeler
Movers, Mines, and Murder (Book 2)
katherinesbooks.com/movers
Lunar Justice (Book 3)
katherinesbooks.com/lunarjustice
Spencer Legacy (Book 4)

katherinesbooks.com/spencerlegacy

ABOUT THE AUTHOR

Katherine is a science fiction author who spent nearly thirty years working as an engineer before retiring and turning to her life-long love of storytelling. She grew up devouring classic sci-fi, especially the works of Isaac Asimov, Arthur C. Clarke, and Ray Bradbury. As much as she adored those stories, she often felt something was missing.

Over time, her reading tastes broadened to include cozy mysteries, thrillers, and fantasy. Eventually she realized her ideal book would be a blend of the genres she loved most. The solution was obvious: write cross-genre stories that fuse the wonder of science fiction with the charm and puzzle-solving of cozy mystery.

Katherine lives in New England, where she spends her days writing, reading, and enjoying time with her family.